POTTERY AND PERPS

A MIRA MICHAELS MYSTERY

JULIA KOTY

BUSSTOP PRESS

Cover design by Kim Thurlow
Book design by Natasha Sass

ISBN 978-1-939309-15-0 (paperback)
ISBN 978-1-939309-16-7 (large print paperback)
ISBN 978-1-939309-14-3 (ebook)
www.JuliaKoty.com

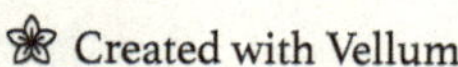 Created with Vellum

1

———

I tried to start my Buick for the fourth time. "Come on Babs," I cajoled. But nothing happened. I stared at the long line at the farm stand.

Mr. Miller called to me over the heads of the customers, "I can take you to the diner; it's not a problem. I'll just close up for a bit."

Kindness under all circumstances was the vibe amongst the people in Pleasant Pond. Except for the occasional murderer, of course.

"I can call a tow; she'll need to get there eventually anyway." I couldn't allow a fellow business owner to shut down his shop when business was hopping. I'd call for a tow, but not from the hot car. I slipped out—the temperature wasn't much different. The summer sun was in its glory today. I quickly searched and dialed the local garage number. No answer.

I slumped against the car. Now what? I could call Jay to verify if I had the right number. It couldn't hurt. Even though I knew he was off-limits—he had a girlfriend—my heart beat a little faster as I pressed the call button next to his name.

"Mira?"

"Hey, Jay. I ran into some car trouble and I'm wondering if you can recommend a tow."

"Sure, it's the place in town. Jasper's Garage."

"I just called there. No one picked up."

"Do you want me to stop by and take you over to the diner?"

"No, it's all right, I'll just call again." I didn't want Jay to leave his work site. Not to help me out of a bind. Even though that seemed like our relationship. My kitchen explodes, Jay fixes it.

"Are you sure? Devon is here. He can take over for me."

I knew Devon from his help with the kitchen renovations. Nice kid. "I'll try calling again. If I have any problems I'll call you back, how's that?"

"Alright, But I'm serious about the help. I'll watch for your call."

I called the garage again. After five rings, someone picked up. "Jasper's Garage. Jasper speaking."

"Hi, Jasper, my car is dead. Can I have a tow? I'm at Miller's farm stand."

I could barely hear Jasper's voice over the bang and clang sounds of a busy garage. "I'll send the truck."

The four gallons of milk and six-dozen eggs I bought at the farm stand would not last long in the heat of the car. I opened up the back door to move them to the shade of Mr. Miller's stand, but before I could haul them out of the backseat, the tow truck arrived. I closed the door and walked away from Babs to greet the driver. When he stepped out of the cab, my mouth gaped open. Wyatt's blond hair was shorter now, but he still had those same dreamy dark blue eyes.

"I know you." He shook a finger at me. "Route 80? Or was it 287?"

"You bought me a new battery," popped out of my surprised mouth.

He gave Babs a concerned look. "I hope it wasn't a bad one?"

"It's been running great. Thanks. But at the time, you mentioned something about the alternator." I stepped aside as he walked to the front of the Buick and opened the driver side door in one swift motion, unlatching the hood.

"It could be." He lifted the hood in a single graceful arc and propped up the support bar. "Do you want to try starting it?"

"Sure." I hopped behind the driver's side door, making sure the emergency brake was on, and started the car. Or tried to. Bab's engine only made a ticking sound.

"You can stop."

I turned off the ignition, got out of the car, walked to the front, and stood next to him. He surveyed the engine block. "Do you know what it is?" I asked.

"I'll test the battery just to be sure, but I think it is the alternator. We can tow it back to Jasper's and take care of it for you."

"This time I can pay for it." I smiled.

"I don't doubt it." He grinned back. "Let's get this baby hooked up."

There were certain benefits to being in the middle of Miller's field. There was enough room to allow the tow truck to drive around Babs and roll back close enough so the winch could pull her up onto the flat bed.

The other benefit was the fresh lemonade that Mr. Miller handed to us once his customers had departed.

"Thanks, Mr. Miller." The tart iced drink hit the spot. I hadn't realized it would be this hot out when I left the diner this morning after we ran out of milk.

I remembered the time we first met as I watched Wyatt sipping his lemonade. "I thought you worked near the Philadelphia area," I said.

"I do. I did. I'm out here helping my cousin Jasper. He needed someone to drive the tow and assist around the shop, so I figured I'd take in the scenery."

"It is definitely quiet here."

"Do you enjoy it?" He asked like maybe he wasn't sure if he liked the quiet.

"Yes. Actually, I do." I took the last sip of my lemonade. "I cook at the diner. You should stop by. I'll buy you some lunch." Maybe I could convince him to stick around. He was just the kind of nice guy I liked to be friends with and I couldn't ignore those dreamy eyes.

"I might just do that." He looked down at his empty cup. "Hey, were you able to find the man that kidnapped the cat?"

"I did. Thanks to your trucker friend's help. We found her and returned the kitty to her owner."

"That's great to hear. I knew you wouldn't give up." His blue eyes twinkled.

I grinned.

"Let's get your Buick over to Jasper and fix her up."

We thanked Mr. Miller for the drinks and walked back to the truck. Wyatt started the engine. As I climbed up into the passenger side of his cab, I imagined finding fast food wrappers, chip bags, or other garbage. Instead, what I saw was a very peaceful, extremely clean, detailed tow truck cab.

Instead of a pine tree deodorant hanging from the rearview, a single crystal on a black silk cord caught the light from the early morning sun. I relaxed.

"I can't lie to you." Wyatt glanced at me as we turned onto the road. "An alternator is not cheap."

"I figured as much." Internally I cringed. Most of the money my ex, Alex, had given to me, or rather, returned to me, had already been paid to Bob at the hardware store for the kitchen appliances. I was just waiting on them to arrive. I didn't have a lot of money to cover car troubles.

"I'll make sure Jasper gives it to you at cost."

"You don't have to do that, Wyatt." I sighed. "I've got the money."

"Jasper and I can give your old girl a good once-over and let you know if anything needs shoring up. More like a wellness check. She is pretty old. You might want to start thinking about investing in something newer."

I noticed he hadn't said new. "Does Jasper sell used cars?"

"He does. I could look into it for you."

"I don't know. Me and Babs have been through a lot."

"I hear you. I had an old clunker once too. Good times." He grinned to himself.

I mentioned the milk and eggs and how they were needed at the diner. Wyatt offered to drop me and the food at the diner. He even helped me carry in the four gallons of milk. I made sure to hand him the keys to Babs. After he said goodbye, Aerie gave me the raised eyebrow. "Who was that?"

THE DINER WAS FULL, but Aerie helped me put everything back into the kitchen. "Well?" She tightened her blond ponytail. "Are you going to tell me, or do I have to drag it out of you?"

"What?" I grinned.

"What happened? Who was that?" She nudged me with her elbow.

"Oh, Babs crashed and burned. I mean not crashed. The alternator is probably dead. And that was Wyatt, he works with Jasper at the garage."

"Do you know each other?" She stressed the word know with a lilt in her voice.

"Believe it or not, I met him on my drive down here in March. He bought me a car battery."

Aerie nodded her head. "He likes you."

"He does not. He's just a really nice guy."

"And a cutie. And a gentleman." She picked up one of the gallons of milk.

"Stop trying to set me up," I reprimanded Aerie.

The bells over the door chimed and, as if on cue, Detective Dan Lockhart graced us with his presence. Mid-giggle, Aerie and I stopped cold and shared a look. Dan walked up and sat at the counter. "Good morning, ladies."

"Good morning, Dan," Aerie and I responded in unison.

Flustered, I ducked back into the kitchen. Things had been weird with Dan ever since the spring. That whole thing with my sister when she prodded him to watch over me. Then he and I attempted to date. But then we didn't date. It was a mess. I didn't know if I was up for the challenge of trying to sort it out. Not right now, anyway. Keeping Dan at arm's length was probably what kept my sanity.

I glanced up at the kitchen chalkboard noticing that

Aerie had managed all of the take-out meals while I was gone. She came in with Dan's order. I dropped a sausage patty on the grill and grabbed two eggs.

"Mrs. Orsa is still out front, so I'm going to visit with her. You got this?"

"Sure." As long as Aerie talked to the customers, I could stay in the kitchen, and it was all good. I cracked the eggs, scrambled them, toasted the English muffin, then put together the breakfast sandwich Dan ordered. I could take it out to him. I was an adult. I didn't have to make small talk. I just needed to hand him his breakfast. I gulped. As I walked around the corner, his phone rang. I thanked the Universe. I slid the glass plate along the counter in front of him.

Dan's eyebrows pinched together, and he leaned back on the stool. "At Spring Creek Plaza? Is everyone else okay? EMTs were sent?" He nodded. "I'll be right over." He stuffed his phone in his back pocket then glanced up at me. "Can I take this to go please?"

"Sure." I wondered what was going on. Obviously, something very serious at the plaza. Aerie overheard as well and made a beeline for Dan. "What happened?"

"Don't worry, Sam is fine. It has nothing to do with the Pizza Pub."

Aerie relaxed with a sigh.

"What happened?" I asked, mostly because I couldn't help it.

Dan gave me a look that I was very familiar with. "I don't need any help, Mira."

I finished wrapping up his sandwich and handed it to him. He pulled out a ten-dollar bill, which I took. I gave him a pleading look.

He sighed. "A body was found at Pocket Moon Pottery in the plaza."

"Is Heather okay?" I had met Heather, the owner, earlier this year.

"Yes. But I can't tell you the person's identity until the family has been notified."

"Understood." I put his money in the register, he turned and left the diner, the bells jingling as the door dropped shut.

Aerie and I both stared at each other. "Obviously, we need to go see if Heather is okay."

"And see what kind of trouble we can get into," Aerie added.

"For someone that wants to see me hooked up with Dan, this idea of yours isn't going to put me in his good graces."

"I know. Half the fun is torturing him."

"I'm all in. But hey, let's do something unique and finish working first."

"Deal. But I'm going to call Sam and find out what he knows."

"Good idea." I wandered back into the kitchen to clean up. We still had the lunch rush to prepare for. We couldn't leave anytime soon, but if she got information out of Sam that would at least keep our curiosity at bay until 2:45.

After waiting a grueling five minutes, Aerie reappeared. "Sam says it was Vicki Hudson that was killed."

Working in the diner allowed me to meet a good number of the residents of Pleasant Pond. But I didn't know everyone, and I had never heard of Vicki Hudson.

"She was a few years younger than me in school. I didn't know her very well. Sam invited us over for lunch when we get off work."

"I was already craving pizza. I planned on having lunch at Sam's even before Dan showed up," I lied.

"Is that so?" Aerie played along. "Me too."

"I guess we'll be going to Sam's after we close up."

"I guess so."

Then I got serious. "Let's prep for lunch, I bet everyone will be stopping by to ask for details." Aerie nodded and went back out front to bus the tables.

I wondered who Vicky was. My mind immediately asked questions about her relationships and why someone would want to kill her in a paint-your-own-pottery shop. Poor Heather. Aerie and I knew all too well the ramifications of a murder on a small business. Barely anyone came to our diner after someone had been poisoned there. But we also knew how to get to the other side. All we needed to do was solve the crime and find the perpetrator.

2

____

A erie and I didn't exactly shove our last customer out the door, but we were pretty impatient for him to leave.

"Jay, can you just take it to go?" Aerie glared at her brother.

"You want to see the body, don't you? The two of you have issues." Jay wiped his lips on the napkin and folded it slowly.

Aerie snatched it from his hands, grabbed his plate and walked back into the kitchen to load and run the final stack of dishes in the dishwasher.

We finished all the closing tasks and headed for the door. Jay, at the last minute, decided to re-tie his boots.

"Don't you have work to do?" Aerie needled him.

"I do. But I promised Dan that I would keep you guys busy so you wouldn't mess up the crime scene."

Aerie let out a screech and threw a dishtowel at him. Both of us shot evil glances in his direction. Aerie snatched the diner keys from my hands, threw them on the counter, and pointed at Jay. "You can close up then."

Aerie and I walked out the door and headed to her car. The hot August day just intensified the fact that we both smelled like fryer oil.

"I can't believe him. Conspiring with Dan to keep us away from the murder scene."

"You and I should know better. Jay and Dan are BFFs." In the rush to leave I'd forgotten to take off my apron. I jerked the ties and dropped it onto the backseat.

It took less than ten minutes to Sam's. We exchanged the scent of fryer grease for pizza-oven as we walked inside. The air conditioning fought to keep the heat down to a manageable level, so we weren't actively sweating inside the restaurant. Sam, on the other hand, was using what looked like five separate fans to keep the air moving in the kitchen.

As per the usual, Aerie walked into the kitchen to greet him while I grabbed a booth in the dining room. As I turned to sit, I noticed someone sitting deep in the corner of a booth in the back of the dining room. It was Heather. I rushed to her and settled in across the table from her. I knew exactly how she felt. The memory of serving supposedly poisoned mushroom soup at the diner this past spring was still fresh in my mind. She looked up from the mug of hot tea she was sipping.

And then I said the stupidest thing. "Are you okay?" Because, of course, she was not.

Heather seemed stunned. "It was the worst thing. Finding her like that, taped to a chair, her eyes staring." She shook her head to clear the image from her mind.

"I can imagine. We will figure out who did it. Aerie and me," I told her.

She took another sip of her tea, swallowed, and stared me straight in the eye. "I can't just sit around and do nothing. I'll help too."

I nodded vigorously. I knew the feeling well.

Aerie slid into the booth next to me. "How can we help you, Heather?"

"Find who did this. Vicki was sweet and one of my best customers."

"Vicki Hudson?"

Heather nodded. "Yes. She had been at the GNO, you know, Girls' Night Out painting party last night. I found her this morning when I opened up."

"Is it possible she never left?"

"I can't see how. I thought the store was empty when I locked up. But it's all a blur now." Heather shook her head.

"Can you walk us through the evening?" I asked her.

Heather finished the last sip of her tea and gently placed the cup on the table. She took a deep breath. "It was your basic BYOB girls' night out. Lots of talking and chatter. Once I got everyone settled down, I walked them through the project."

"What did you paint?" Aerie had been wanting to paint at the pottery place for weeks now. We just couldn't find the time. Running a diner and solving murders kept us busy.

"A basic platter. We painted a beach scene on the face of it."

"Oh, that sounds nice." I shot Aerie a pleading glance. "Right. Stick to questions that related to the murder."

"Vicki was there?"

Heather nodded. "She was with the rest of her girlfriends. Everything was going well until some kind of fight broke out between her and Tayla. Vicki got really upset and started screaming at her, and then Tayla started yelling at Vicki. Because everyone had been drinking, it escalated."

"Did you need to call the police?"

Heather shook her head. "I almost did. But no. Tayla's

brother is Tyler Stewart." Tyler was an officer on the force who worked with Dan. "As soon as I mentioned phoning someone, the disagreement stopped. The party never recovered after that."

"Do you remember what they argued about?"

"I think Tayla dripped paint on Vicki's painting. At least that's how it started. By the end of it, both platters were a mess of paint until Tayla picked up Vicki's and smashed it on the floor."

"Did you threaten to call the police when she threw the platter?"

"Yes. The last thing I wanted was a fight with more broken pottery. But Tayla ended up paying for it. I thought it was all finished, but then..." Heather's eyes filled with tears and I imagined she was remembering finding Vicki's body this morning.

"Do you have a list of everyone that attended the party?"

Heather nodded. "Each attendee needs to fill out an order form. I gave Detective Lockheart the originals, but I have all of it in the computer. I can print them out for you, if you'd like."

"Sure, but I'm guessing we're not allowed in your shop yet."

Heather pulled out her phone. "I have access to the app from here. We just need to find a printer to send it to."

Sam placed glasses of ice water on the table. "I can help with that. There's a printer in my office."

"Thanks, Sam." Aerie hopped up and kissed him on the cheek.

We followed Aerie into the kitchen and made a left into a small room that was Sam's office. The tiny space felt like a sauna. But after printing out the list of partygoers, we chugged the last of the water and finished our lunch. Heather managed to nibble on a slice of cheese pizza.

"Heather, do you want to come back to my house? You could play with Ozzie and take a break from all of this?" I asked.

She looked up from her tea mug and her mood seemed to clear. "You know what? Yes, I think that would help. I always wanted to know how you both managed these investigations."

I glanced at Aerie who silently agreed. "We'll show you how we work." I slid out of the booth, my sweaty legs sticking to the vinyl.

Aerie cleared her throat. "As long as you don't mind a bit of craziness, then we're good."

"OKAY GUYS, watch out for the stampede," I announced as I put the key in the door. Sure enough, Ozzie galloped through the dining room. If she had been a bigger dog, she would have taken us all out. But being the tiny terrier that she was, our shins just took a battering. Taco the scarlet macaw made sure he was heard as well. Even though his cage was in the far corner of the room, he squawked, "Welcome to the Cantina. Welcome to the Cantina." Taco had a colorful background; I inherited him from a prior investigation. Like my fish, and the mice that, thankfully, Aerie took. Between the two of us we could start a zoo, or an animal sanctuary.

Arnold sat primly off to the side with his front paws tightly together, overseeing the chaos. *Must there be so much madness every time the door opens?*

He got grumpy waiting for kitty treats. I wondered if he

was happy I was home, or if it was just because that was when he got his kitty treats.

Both.

I gave him a grin with a little bit of side-eye for his snark. I opened the drawer to the small desk near the front door and pulled out the kitty treats. The bag made a crinkling sound. Arnold's eyes locked on target and didn't leave until he was munching a treat between his teeth. Ozzie, on the other hand, could live on petting alone, or at least it appeared that way.

"Come on in. The living room has a nicely worn couch. Very comfortable. I'll get us some sodas." I walked into the newly drywalled kitchen. It was still just a box. No cupboards, no appliances, just a gas connection and a couple of electrical outlets. For a moment, I wondered if I would actually be able to afford fixing the car after I just bought the much-needed appliances. I picked up the box fan at the far end of the kitchen and pushed open the front window. This new window slid up easily compared to the ancient windows in the rest of the house.

"Aerie? Feel free to turn on the fans in the living room." Without AC my Victorian got downright hot in the summer. The idea of adding central air conditioning to the hundred and fifty-year-old house wasn't even a consideration. Any money I had, as little as it was, had to go toward necessary renovations. I took a deep sigh. And now the car. I wondered how Wyatt was doing with Babs.

I grabbed three watermelon flavored sodas out of the tiny dorm refrigerator and headed to the living room.

Aerie had turned on the fans, but the room still felt like a warm bread box. I handed out the cans of soda. "I think if we open the back door, it might help get some air going." I unlocked and opened both the porch and house doors. This helped infinitesimally and for a moment I wondered if all three of us could fit on the porch swing.

"I was just explaining to Heather how we go about figuring these things out."

"Did you leave out the good parts like the sprained ankle and the arrest warrant and..."

Aerie winced. "Each one is different. Plus, I didn't want to scare her."

Heather tucked her dress under her as she sat on the couch, her lilac combat boots coordinated with the floral pattern. "You can't scare me, Aerie. I just want to find out who did this. Who would come into my shop and do something so horrible? I want to make sure they see justice."

Aerie and I nodded in agreement. Not too long ago when our own business was threatened, we dealt with the challenges and the desperate need for justice.

"The first thing we do is we create a list of potential suspects."

"This list is a great start." Aerie pointed to the printout. She read through the list and then made a sour face.

"What is it?" I asked her.

"Chelsea is on here." Aerie's bitter look was a reminder that her childhood bully was still a sore spot for her.

"Chelsea Smith was at the party last night?" I asked. She was also Jay's girlfriend so there was no love lost from me either.

Heather nodded.

"She wasn't in the fight?" Aerie asked as if she was surprised. To be honest, so was I.

Heather thought a moment. "Not directly. But I don't remember her trying to calm anything down either."

Aerie nodded knowingly. Her glance fell on me. "You get to interview her."

"Why me?" I asked.

"I hate her more than you do," she said.

"Fine," I said. Aerie handed me the list of names. I read through the list quickly. "Josie Colts, Mia Olsen, Sophia Malden, Gloria Boyer, Anita Buss, Stacy Morgan. Most of these women work at the newspaper."

"It looks like our first step is to visit the Pleasant Pond Independent."

Aerie turned to Heather. "That's how we take our first step in the plan."

"Do you guys mind if I tag along? I need to do something. I can't go back to the shop."

"We would be happy to have you join us. The more the merrier," Aerie said.

"I don't know about merrier, but we can definitely use the help," I added.

We talked a little bit more about how we interview people and we reassured Heather that we would find who had done this.

"Somehow we always manage to figure it out in the end," I told her.

"Even if there's a bit of chaos." Aerie giggled.

A huge crash sounded from the kitchen. I jumped up. The three of us searched in the direction of the crash. My immediate thought was that Arnold or Ozzie had gotten into something trying to get a hold of treats. But when we arrived in the kitchen, the box fan was lying on the floor and the window was closed. I stared at it for a moment recalling I had put the fan in the window.

"That's odd. I remember opening this window."

I picked up the fan. Aerie pushed up the window and I set it back on the ledge. I shrugged. Had I remembered wrong? Had I turned on the fan in the windowsill but hadn't actually opened the window? It would definitely have fallen over if that was the case. I shrugged again and led everyone out of the kitchen.

We finished our drinks in the dining room.

"I think one of our first steps should be to interview the women at the newspaper office."

"That way we can talk to everyone together and see what we can learn."

I looked at my phone. "It's after 4:30. They will have closed up by now and gone home for the weekend."

"The newspaper won't open till Monday. We could locate and interview each woman separately too," Heather offered.

"First thing tomorrow," Aerie said. "Heather needs some rest."

My heart sank. "Guys, tomorrow Jay is coming over to paint the kitchen. I promised I would help."

Aerie patted me on the back. "No problem. Heather and I can fill you in on what we find out."

3

———

The next morning, I woke to the sharp poke of Arnold's claw jabbing the hollow in my exposed neck. I pushed his paw away. "Arnold, that is the meanest way to wake someone up."

It is the most effective way. It works almost instantly when I have my claw on your jugular.

"Can you stop doing that?"

Not likely. As I said, it's effective. I'm hungry.

Ozzie let out an impatient whine from the floor at the side of the bed. I would need to take her for a quick walk before Jay got here.

I wondered what Heather and Aerie would learn without me. I was super curious and a little upset that I couldn't join them. However, the prospect of spending the morning with Jay, alone, painting the kitchen, wasn't so bad.

Taking care of Arnold and Ozzie was a routine that was relatively quick and easy. So was feeding the two koi fish. Taco was always a bit of a challenge. I was under the impression that he hadn't stayed inside a cage most of his life. Every time I opened the door, he hopped on my arm and tried to make his way out. This morning he tried especially hard. I kept maneuvering myself to block the open door to his cage, but he still escaped. Mostly because I was afraid of his sharp beak, and I flinched when he got close to me. Taco burst out of the cage with a loud squawk, flew in a giant arc around the room, and perched himself on top of the card table I used as a dining room table. He puffed out his chest. "Taco, touchdown! Taco, touchdown!"

There was a knock at the door.

It had to be Jay. "Come in." I shouted.

He peeked his head around the door. "Okay, to enter?"

"Yes, I'm just dealing with Taco here." I sent a seething glance at the bird. "Bad bird."

"Taco, touchdown. Touchdown!" His squawking reverberated throughout the house. Arnold hissed and ran upstairs.

"I think he lived in a bar or a restaurant or something," I muttered.

"Really? Why do you think so?"

"You should hear some of his more colorful phrases." I inched my way closer to Taco so he wouldn't take flight again. Trying not to look at his claws.

Jay grinned and my heart melted. Taco squawked again and I regained my composure.

"Let me put him back in the cage before he gets into more trouble."

"Do you want any help?" Jay looked at the bird warily.

I noticed Jay held two gallons of paint. "It's okay. I can manage. Um, you can put the cans in the kitchen." I took a deep breath. I needed Jay to leave the room so I wouldn't be mortified while I attempted to get Taco to obey. Because there was only one way to get the bird to follow me to his cage.

At first, I tried the regular way of asking Taco nicely. "Come on Taco, let's go." I waved my hand. "Come on boy, back in the cage."

He moved from the table to the top of the chair closest to me, and I actually had the nerve to think this was working. "Come on birdy. Let's go in."

Taco let out a bone reverberating squawk that made my ears ring. "Give Taco a kiss. Give Taco a kiss."

There was no denying that Jay had heard it. He walked out of the kitchen and back into the dining room. I couldn't turn around and let him see how red my face was with embarrassment; I felt it like a hot wave of sheer mortification.

There was no helping it. I needed to get Taco back in the cage so I could help Jay. I sighed. "Come here Taco, I'll give you a kiss."

Taco hopped onto my wrist. If I didn't follow through, he'd fly back to the table and we'd have to start all over again. I knew from experience. I felt Jay's eyes watching me. I leaned down and kissed Taco on his beak.

"Kachow!" Taco replied.

I shook my head and turned toward the open cage door. Taco stepped off my wrist and onto his perch inside his cage.

I turned around to find Jay grinning ear to ear.

"What was that?"

Flustered, I could barely breathe let alone form words. I waved my hands.

Jay held back his laughter and simply grinned wider. I followed him into the kitchen.

"I stopped by Bob's hardware store and picked up the paint. The color looks pretty good. Nice choice."

"Thanks." I had chosen a very pale yellow for the

kitchen. I was surprised how excited I was to start painting and making the kitchen feel homier.

I noticed a canvas bag with a pole and rollers. Jay grabbed the bag and carried it over. "I brought rollers so between the two of us we should get this done in an hour or two. Cake."

"Sounds good." I watched Jay pry open the lid on one of the cans of paint and pour the soft yellow liquid into the tray. Yep, I was excited to get started.

Jay paused and looked at me. "Is that what you're going to wear?"

I looked at my outfit, an old T-shirt and sweatpants. "Yeah. Something wrong?"

"No, um, you look nice. Do you have a hat?"

"Hat?" I didn't understand where the conversation was going. Jay took off his baseball cap and dropped it on my head. "You can wear mine. You don't want paint on that beautiful curly hair of yours. It would take forever to get out."

I blushed again. I felt the warmth of Jay's hat when I pushed my hair up under its protection.

An awkward silence hung over the room as he went to work. I had only ever painted my own bedroom when I was sixteen. So, I wasn't quite sure if I was doing it right but I was too nervous to ask Jay.

"Do you want some help with that?"

"What?" I turned and felt it before I saw it. A huge dollop of yellow dropped from my roller onto the top of my bare foot. My mouth gaped open. I stared down at the mess on my toes.

"I was going to mention you had too much paint on your roller." Jay grinned.

"Yeah." I continued to stare at my foot. Jay pulled a roll

of paper towels from the canvas bag and tore off a piece. For a moment it looked like he was going to lean down and clean off my toes for me. But instead, he handed me the paper towel and took the paint-laden roller from my hand and put it back in the paint tray.

I cleaned off my toes as best I could. "Thanks. It's been a while since I did this."

"No worries; it's just paint. You have to roll the roller in the tray a little bit to get the excess paint off." He demonstrated and then handed me the roller. "And then you want to roll it like this." He picked up his and demonstrated, rolling the paint back and forth along the wall in an X pattern. I followed his lead and rolled Xs across the white drywall.

Jay focused on the areas near the ceiling. We continued this way for a while. He was definitely faster than I was, and soon the top area of the walls was a soothing yellow. "I have a ladder in my truck. I'll cut in the edging with a brush."

"Sounds good." I continued to pick up paint, roll it in the tray, and apply it to the wall with rhythmic Xs.

Jay returned, but he was on the phone. "I don't want to talk about it right now. I'm on a job. Fine, we can talk about it tonight." He ended the call and stuffed the phone into his back pocket. "Sorry about that. Chelsea." He said it as if her name alone was enough to explain.

"It's okay. Sorry you guys are having an argument."

"Oh, it's not an argument really."

I didn't want to get in the middle. I disliked Chelsea and, at the same time, had a crush on Jay that just wouldn't go away.

"Chelsea says she wants to have kids right away." Jay shook his head.

My stomach dropped. "But you two aren't married." I blurted it out before I even thought about it.

"That's what I said." He seemed happy to have someone agree with him. "She told me she doesn't care." He paused for a moment and then climbed the ladder. "But, like, I care."

I nodded and focused on the walls. A minute later, Jay changed the subject. "Are you and Aerie working on the murder at Pocket Moon Pottery?"

"Does everybody think that we automatically investigate every crime in town?"

Jay laughed. "Yeah. I think so."

"Heather asked us to help. She says it's driving her crazy to sit in the shop and not know what's happening with the investigation."

"It's insane. The whole thing. Chelsea was even there the night it happened."

"She was?" I totally faked that I didn't already know.

"Yeah, she's friends with Tayla and Mia, who work over at the paper."

"I think Aerie and Heather are heading out today to ask some questions." I mentioned.

"I won't tell Dan."

I gave him the side eye. "Yeah, right, just yesterday you were working for him to keep us from leaving the diner to get to the scene."

"It doesn't bother me either way. If Dan asks me for a favor, I do it. If you ask me for a favor, I do it. And if they clash I'll let you do it yourselves."

"That's an interesting way of playing the fence."

Jay shrugged. "A man's gotta stay alive." He coughed. "So to speak."

Jay was on the ladder painting near the ceiling, cutting in the edges when Taco squawked behind me and made me jump out of my skin.

I turned and gave him a dirty look. "Quiet." Taco squawked again. I went over to his cage to check on him. He seemed more agitated than usual. But then I hadn't had him very long; maybe he was just lonely.

"How's it going, buddy?" I asked him.

He let out a generic squawk that made my teeth rattle. He began to preen his feathers and ignored me.

A crash came from the kitchen, and I ran to see if Jay was okay. I spotted him on the ladder twisting around to look at the window. The box fan was flat on the floor with the window closed.

"Again?" I stared at the fan.

"That's happened before?" Jay climbed down from the ladder.

"Yeah, I guess the window pushes the fan out and it falls on the floor."

"It's a new window. It should stay up where you prop it. But I'll check it out for you before I leave."

We pushed the window open, propped the fan back in, and securely pressed the bottom of the window to the top of the fan so the handle could keep it from falling again. I shook my head and we went back to painting.

Jay and I had an easy and comfortable conversation. We did not discuss either Dan or Chelsea.

Just before he left, Jay checked the window. "I can't find anything wrong with it. But if it keeps happening, let me know and I can talk to someone over at the general contractor site and see if I can get you a new window. Which reminds me, we are demo-ing an old kitchen up on Oak Street. I was wondering if maybe you would want the cabinets?"

"Cabinets?"

"You can have them for free. They would just end up in the dumpster otherwise."

"Really?" I couldn't contain my enthusiasm for free cabinets.

"Yeah, they're in decent shape. We can paint them whatever color you want. I can bring them by later this week once they're out."

"Jay, that's awesome. Thank you." I could almost hug and kiss him. But I stopped myself. "I don't know what I would do without you," I told him.

"Yeah, tell that to— Never mind. I'll see you later in the week."

When the fan fell on the floor for the second time, I closed my eyes. "Clara?" The ghost of the house remained silent.

4

The house still smelled of fresh paint when the doorbell rang. Aerie stepped into the front room. "Well, it wasn't as productive as we would've hoped," she said.

Heather followed her inside. "Gloria, from the newspaper, was the only one home today."

Aerie waved her hand near her face. "Whew, it smells like paint in here. Did you and Jay finish the kitchen?"

"Yep, do you guys want to see it?" As much as I wanted to hear what they learned I was excited to show off my kitchen walls.

Aerie and Heather followed me toward the entrance.

"I like the yellow; nice choice," Aerie said.

Heather nodded. "Beautiful color."

"Actually, Jay says they may have some cabinets for me that they are taking out of a new worksite."

"This is suddenly making me want to repaint a room in my house," Heather said. "It would keep my mind off of everything."

"What did you guys find out?" I grabbed an extra folding chair for Heather, and we sat at the card table.

"The first thing we learned was that Gloria does not relish her husband's retirement." Aerie settled in and put her hands softly on the tabletop.

"I think if the newspaper ran seven days a week instead of six, she would be there."

"But what did you learn about the murder?"

"Yeah, that's the thing. Not that much. Gloria saw the argument. She says it looked like two catty millennials crying to each other. She said she refused to spend too much time paying attention to that nonsense."

"That's it?"

Heather nodded. "Yes, she couldn't add anything more than I had seen of the argument. Except her colorful opinion."

"Did you try to find any of the other women today?"

"I figure I can talk to Sophia at yoga tomorrow morning. Chelsea is a friend of Mia and Vicki. So far, she's avoiding us, we think."

Heather nodded. "We stopped by the general store to look for Stacy but she wasn't available. Anita, who owns the B&B, is on the list, but we didn't get a chance to ride out there yet."

"It's a start, I suppose." I said.

"A slow one."

"What about Chelsea?" I asked.

"I told you, she's all yours." Aerie glared at me.

"Fine. I'll hunt her down." I internally cringed.

"Heather, you'll have to pardon me while I grill Mira about Jay." Aerie looked me in the eye. "Have you been able to seduce him away from Chelsea yet?"

"What are you talking about?"

"She's making him miserable, it's obvious. So, have you taken advantage of that and made your move?"

I shook my head. "Aerie. You're crazy. You've been trying to set me up with every man on two feet in this town. Especially your brother." She waited patiently, looking at me expectantly. "He came over. We painted the walls and chatted. The fan fell out of the window and when we finished painting Jay went home."

The doorbell rang.

A deliveryman dressed in brown held a small box. "Delivery for Mira Michaels?"

"That's me." Although, I had no idea who would send me a package. I hadn't ordered anything. But once I took it, I noticed the return address. Darla Damian, Stoneport, Massachusetts. "What is this?" I mumbled under my breath.

"I don't know. You'll have to open it up and find out," the delivery guy responded in a chipper voice. "Have a good day."

"Thanks." I stared at the box as I closed the door. What was my sister sending me?

Aerie giggled. "He's good looking."

"Are you going to set me up with the delivery guy too?"

"Maybe."

Taco squawked extremely loudly in the corner and all three of us jumped in our chairs. "He's a player. He's a player."

"That bird. He's going to drive me to drink."

Aerie looked at Taco. "Who's a player, Taco?"

"He's a player. He's a player."

"Aerie, don't play along with him. I'm trying to get him to talk less, not more." I rubbed the goosebumps on my arms. "Between him and the fan falling out of the window, I'm on my last nerve."

"What do you mean 'the fan falls out of the window'?"

"I don't know. Jay looked at it and says he can't find anything wrong with the window but for some reason it keeps closing and pushing the fan onto the floor." I pointed toward the kitchen. Aerie stepped in there to get a good look.

"To tell you the truth, Aerie..." I shot a side glance at Heather. She had to learn at some point how crazy my life was. "I'm wondering if it's Clara."

"The ghost that lives here?"

"Yeah. When Darla visited earlier this month, she did her psychic mumbo jumbo and mentioned something about Clara needing my help. I'm guessing she's letting me know."

"I have a ghost in my house, too," Heather said.

Aerie and I stopped and turned. "You do?" we asked in unison.

"Yep. Whoever it is, he or she likes to rearrange everything in my bathroom. I can never find the lipstick that I want, and my shoes are always paired up in different ways. A real jokester, my ghost."

I rubbed the goosebumps on my arms again. Even though the room was very warm, the goosebumps wouldn't go away. "Let's change the subject. What's our plan to interview the other women who attended the party?"

"Like I said, I can check on Sophia when she visits yoga tomorrow morning. But then I suppose we should make a trip over to the newspaper office on Monday morning."

"That sounds like a plan," I said.

"Are you okay, Heather?" Aerie asked.

"Sure. I'm glad I could do something today. Is it okay if I still tag along with you guys?"

"Of course. We will be working tomorrow morning for

Sunday brunch. But why don't we try to visit the general store and talk to Stacy."

"Okay. Thanks for having me, guys. I'll see you later tomorrow." Heather stood.

"Heather, we'll figure this out, don't worry," I told her.

She nodded and left.

"We'll figure it out," I said this more to myself than anything.

"We always do," Aerie said. "What's this box?"

"Oh, something from Darla." I shrugged.

Taco squawked again, "He's a player."

"Ugh." I rolled my eyes. "I need to find a new home for Taco."

"Aw, you don't want to keep this guy?" Aerie walked to his cage.

"Sexy lady. Sexy lady."

Aerie pinched her lips together. "I see what you mean."

"Let's go to Sam's, I want to try one of his calzones."

"I got him to add chopped salads to the menu." Aerie rubbed her hands together.

A crash resounded from the kitchen. Aerie and I found the fan on the floor and the window firmly closed.

SUNDAY BRUNCH WAS a little slower than usual. The heat kept people away. Aerie and I had set up fans to push the hot air out of the kitchen, but it still seemed to seep into the dining room making it less than ideal to enjoy a peaceful meal.

I kept the back door to the kitchen open and a fan pointed directly at my face, and I still felt like a baked ham.

Aerie and I were discussing our plans to interview more suspects with Heather this afternoon when Dan showed up for breakfast. I wanted to prove to myself that I could have a practical conversation with him, without embarrassing myself, so I walked out to the counter to say good morning. He looked well put together in his chambray button-down, and with a new haircut too. "How is the investigation going?"

Dan glanced up from his phone. "Are you planning on helping?"

So much for attempting a civil conversation. I erased the smile from my face. "I can't help if I learn things."

Now Dan grinned. "I think you put yourself in a position to learn things."

Maybe he was in a good and sharing mood. "Do you have any suspects?"

"If I did, I wouldn't be able to share them with you." His light tone was so frustrating.

"I figured," I grumbled. "What would you like for breakfast?"

"How about one of your famous breakfast sandwiches? If you wouldn't mind; I know how hot it is."

"The grill is already on, no worries. I'll be right back with your sandwich."

The bells over the door rang as Heather entered. She looked like she hadn't slept.

"Cup of coffee, Heather?" Aerie asked.

Heather just nodded and sat at the counter next to Dan. They mumbled good mornings to each other.

By the time I came back out with Dan's sandwich, he and Heather were deep in conversation.

"I'm sure we can solve this situation, Heather. As we've seen in the past, before you know it, your business will be back up and running. Right Aerie?" Dan asked.

"Absolutely. Heather, this is just a drop in the pan."

Heather shook her head. "It's more than that. Vicki was one of my regulars. She came three nights a week and we chatted. I know I didn't know her like a real friend but I feel like I've lost one."

Aerie came up behind Heather and rubbed her back. "We'll find out who did this."

She glanced up at Dan who nodded. I would take that as acceptance for Aerie and I to help with the case.

I grabbed one of the coffeepots and refilled Dan's mug. "Thanks, Mira."

"No problem." The bells rang over the door again and Wyatt Holland stepped into the dining room.

"Good morning." He was in a chipper mood, sun-kissed but not overheated.

I almost splashed coffee on myself. "Hey, Wyatt what can I get you?"

"I'll tell you what *I* can get *you*. Your car is ready. I finished it this morning."

"It's Sunday. You didn't have to do it today!"

"You're working today."

"It's just brunch," I admitted.

"It's just your car. I know you could use it."

"Thanks, Wyatt. I appreciate it. Do you want some coffee?"

"Sure. Decaf?"

"Not a problem." I put the coffeepot that I was currently holding back and reached for the orange-topped decaf pot while pulling out a mug from the dishwasher tray on the back counter. I slid the mug in front of him and poured a three-quarter cup. "What did you have to do?" I was secretly hinting at how much it would set me back.

"You're free and clear. You just had a couple loose wires. I replaced them and you should be good to go."

"Really." I narrowed my eyes. "It's not something bigger and you paid for it without telling me?"

"Would I do that?"

I gave him a seriously questioning look. "I don't believe you."

He grinned. He had surprisingly beautiful teeth. "All I can say is, your car is ready to go."

"Then breakfast is on me. What can I get you?"

Wyatt clapped his hands together and rubbed them in anticipation. "Let's see, how about the breakfast platter? Some bacon with scrambled eggs and a piece of white toast with butter and maybe some jelly."

"I can manage that." I smiled and realized out of the corner of my eye that Dan was glaring at him.

Wyatt appeared to notice and reached out his hand. "Hey, good morning. Name's Wyatt Holland. I'm working over at Jasper's garage. He's my cousin."

Dan gave him a scrutinizing glare but shook his hand anyway. "Nice to meet you. I'm Dan Lockhart, Chief of Police."

Wyatt appeared surprised and shook Dan's hand harder. "Nice to meet you." Oh boy, the testosterone! I disappeared into the kitchen.

As I whipped up the eggs for Wyatt's scramble, I heard Dan's cell phone vibrate on the counter.

"Yep. I'll be right there," he said. "Send backup." I watched Dan get up from his stool and place a twenty on the counter. "Thank you, ladies, for a wonderful breakfast. Duty calls." He was out the door before we could ask him anything about the call he received. But I did notice that he drove in the direction of Spring Creek Plaza.

Heather noticed as well. "I think I'm going to go check on my shop."

The quick look Aerie gave me didn't really need a response, but I responded anyway. "Go. I'll hold down the diner."

Aerie and Heather bolted out the door. What I wouldn't give to go with them. But Wyatt sat innocently at the counter waiting on his breakfast. So, I stayed and cooked. I just hoped I wouldn't miss anything. Within moments I watched two police cars, lights flashing sirens blaring, fly past the diner toward the plaza. I brought Wyatt's breakfast out to him and placed it neatly on the counter.

"I can take this to go if you want to leave."

I was torn between my good hostess at the diner persona and my private investigator side. Wyatt had been so sweet, he probably paid for whatever my car needed to be fixed, yet here he was telling me it was okay to leave. But I just couldn't stand it. I had to see what was going on.

"I owe you one, Wyatt. Actually, three at this point."

"I'll take a rain check."

I snatched up a takeout container. I gently slid his eggs and bacon and toast inside. When he tried to pay me, I reminded him, "It's on me, Wyatt, thank you."

"No problem. See you later, Mira."

I quickly turned off everything in the kitchen, hung up my apron, grabbed the keys and my phone, and was right behind Wyatt when I locked the diner door. Then reality hit me. I didn't have a car.

A quick glance along the street and I found that Wyatt had driven my car and parked in front of the diner. I watched as he walked down the street back towards the garage.

"You're awesome, Wyatt Holland," I shouted to him.

He just chuckled and kept walking.

$$5$$

I arrived in time to witness Dan escorting a handcuffed man into a squad car. The plate glass window of Pocket Moon Pottery was shattered, and from the mess of broken shards and pottery dust on the floor, it appeared that the man in the squad car had destroyed most of the pottery inside.

Heather was rather stoic about the damage, but Aerie was practically in tears. I caught up with them as they stood outside on the sidewalk looking in.

"Heather, I'm so sorry."

She pinched her lips and nodded.

We were allowed inside once all the photography was completed.

"We'll help you clean it up," Aerie said. "We can get a couple brooms and we can clean this place up good as new."

Heather nodded again and silently picked through the broken pottery. She glanced over our shoulders to see that Dan was occupied. "I need to get to the bottom of this. I want to find her killer."

"Don't worry, we've got Dan; we know how to handle him," Aerie said.

"It's only me he likes to put in jail," I joked.

"I'm heading over to Sam's to get his broom and dustpan, and some garbage bags. I'll be right back."

After Aerie left, I asked Heather, "Who was it that they arrested?"

"Kurt Hudson, Vicki's husband. Maybe this is his way of grieving?" Heather dusted off some of the larger pieces of pottery.

I picked up another broken platter. "Or finishing what he started?"

"Do you think so?"

"It's a possibility. Aerie and I like to keep an open mind until we have all the information."

Aerie came back with a broom, a push mop, and a handful of garbage bags. "What information?"

"I was explaining that we try to keep an open mind about the possible suspects until we have more information."

"Yeah, we need to interview more people. Kurt did this?" Aerie shook her head. "We'll need to talk to him."

"Do you know Kurt Hudson?" I asked Aerie.

"No. I don't. Vicky only came to the diner a few times that I can recall. Never with her husband."

"But Heather, you said she was a regular. Did the two of you talk?"

"We talked all the time. She was an excellent painter." Heather reached up to a platter that teetered on a shelf. The corner now had a ragged chip out of it, but the painting on it, a sunset, was beautiful. "This was one of her projects. When I told her how much I liked it, she gave it to me. It's been in the shop since then." Heather wiped a sleeve across the dusty platter, polishing it gently.

"Did you guys talk about anything more personal? Was she having problems with her husband?"

"We talked about art, pottery, or just random things going on around town. The weather. Nothing important."

"Sometimes it's the small things that can be important clues."

Aerie pushed the dry mop across the floor, and I crouched with the dustpan to scoop up the broken pottery. Heather went to her desk. "I'm going to call the insurance company. I want to get that done. Thank you, guys, but you don't have to stay."

"You're welcome to come back to the diner and have lunch," Aerie added.

"Thanks. I think I want to spend some time here and slowly clean everything up by myself."

"If you need us for anything, let us know. Okay?" I gave her arm a squeeze.

"Sure thing." She managed a small smile. "I just need some time to myself."

Aerie and I both understood the time needed to process everything. Although we had each other to lean on when we dealt with the poisoning at the diner.

We walked outside.

"Do you think it's odd she wanted to be by herself?" I spoke in hushed tones, hoping my voice didn't carry through the broken window.

"No. I mean, look what happened to her shop. I imagine she needs some time alone."

"Maybe I'm just being overly suspicious, trying to guess everyone's ulterior motives," I said.

"It's part of the job with all this investigating that we've been doing. We're constantly trying to figure out why people do things. But don't forget to pay attention to your intuition. That hunch you get."

"You're right." I nodded. Aerie was great at reminding me not to doubt myself.

"Heather really needs our help."

"And that's what were here for. Let's head back to my house and figure out our next steps."

"Do you think you can sweet talk Dan into letting you interview Kurt?"

The look I gave her should have wilted the stoutest of hearts. Aerie just giggled and giggled.

AFTER AERIE and I left Heather, we decided we'd talk to Stacy Morgan, who managed the General Store. She had been at the party and might have some additional information to share. We hoped.

I decided I'd buy Arnold some more kitty treats while I was there. He had had a lot to deal with over the last few months, from a new doggy friend, whom he tolerated, to Taco the obnoxious macaw, whom he couldn't tolerate because the bird was just so crazy loud. I suppose I should be grateful he wasn't actively hunting the fish. Arnold deserved a nice treat.

"Do you know Stacy well?" I asked Aerie. I had only met her a handful of times; I didn't know her personally.

"She's very sweet. She loves her cats."

I nodded in agreement. There was always a cat or two wandering the aisles of the store. And the aisles held more variations on cat treats than you would expect in a small local grocer.

When we arrived, Stacy was busy checking out customers so Aerie followed me back to the aisle with the pet food. This entire side was dedicated to cat toys, cat treats, and cat beds. I could definitely find something that Arnold would enjoy here. I chose a mega container of cat treats, but he deserved something more. Arnold already had a heating mat in his bed, which I knew he found very cozy. A stack of fluffy shaggy cat beds was stacked next to the shelf. I chose what I hoped was Arnold's favorite type, cozy. One of Stacy's cats rubbed against my shin as if approving.

"Splurging on Arnold, are you?" Aerie eyed the cat bed.

"Yeah, he's had to deal with a lot lately."

Aerie nodded. "Between all the animals and the ghost, I can imagine."

"Do not remind me about the ghost." Exasperation didn't cover my feelings on this topic.

"Darla did say you had to help her, soon."

I sighed. "How am I supposed to do that? I don't know the first thing about helping a ghost."

"We could figure it out together." Aerie rubbed her hands.

"You would help me with that?"

"Of course. Helping a ghost sounds exciting." Aerie was always up for something new.

I remembered the package I received from Darla. I still hadn't opened it yet. I had no idea what she sent me. But knowing her it would be something woo-woo.

"Come on, I think I saw Anita in here too." Aerie took the kitty treats from me and we headed over to the checkout. I shifted the cat bed on my hip.

When we got there, Anita was talking with Stacy. Anita owned a bed-and-breakfast in an old Victorian farmhouse on the property adjacent to the Millers.

As we approached the counter, I heard Stacy mention Tayla's name but then they both abruptly stopped talking when they saw us.

I placed the bed on the counter. Aerie dropped the bag of treats next to it. "Good afternoon."

"Are the two of you looking into the murder at Heather Gerry's shop?"

"We are." I could tell they wanted to talk about it.

"I told you we should have gone to the male revue that night," Anita told Stacy.

Stacy nodded. "You're right. You're right. Next time I will listen to you. Because pottery was not as relaxing as one would expect."

"We only heard a little about what happened that night. There was an argument?" I coaxed.

"You could tell those two girls were going to get into a fight at some point in the evening," Anita began.

Stacy nodded. "You could cut the tension with a knife, and then after a couple glasses of wine..."

"Stacy and I just sat there waiting for something to happen and sure enough..."

"Yep, Tayla Stewart was the first to snap. She poked Vicki with her paintbrush. Didn't she?"

"She did. I saw it." Anita nodded.

"And then she spread paint all over Vicki's beautiful painting."

"Vicki was always very proud of her paintings."

"She was. Maybe that's what set Tayla off."

"*You* know that's not why Tayla got mad." Anita gave Stacy a knowing look.

"But I don't think it's for us to say..."

Both women went silent. Aerie and I glanced at each other. "Is there some juicy gossip about Tayla?"

Anita shook her head.

"It's not for us to tell," Stacy added.

Stacy pinched her lips closed and Anita shook her head. It was obvious we weren't getting any more information out of them, at least not about Tayla.

I decided it was best to just come right out and ask. "Do you think Tayla would kill Vicki?"

The women looked at each other and came to a silent agreement that they absolutely believed Tayla could have killed Vicki.

"Why do you think Tayla would do such a thing?"

"You might want to ask Vicki's husband." Stacy rang up my purchases and changed the subject. "This is going to be one happy kitty."

"He deserves it," I said.

"Don't they all. Such loves," Stacy nodded.

Outside the store, Aerie cleared her throat. "They know more than they were telling."

"That's for sure. I guess our next step is to see what Kurt has told Dan." I couldn't wait to hear what reason he gave for trashing Pocket Moon Pottery.

"We can also talk to Tayla. But all of that can happen tomorrow. Ozzie could probably use a walk." Aerie was right.

"If you want, you can stay for dinner."

"Yes, I want to see if Clara shows up." Aerie giggled.

"I'm going to focus on making dinner and building a suspect list; you can play ghostbusters all you want."

6

———

After dinner we decided to check on Heather at her pottery shop because a text to her found that she hadn't gone home yet.

"I just want to make sure she's okay," Aerie said as we got into my car. "We left her in a mess."

I looked around and realized I had left the cat treats and the kitty bed from earlier. Poor Arnold, overlooked again due to all the drama. Then I realized the interior of the car looked substantially cleaner. Certainly better than it had the other day. It took me a second to realize what happened. "Speaking of messes, I think Wyatt cleaned the inside of my car, too."

"He what?" Aerie looked around. "I think you're right. It smells nicer in here too."

I grinned and put the key in the ignition.

"I think he likes you." The lilt in Aerie's voice made me laugh.

"Stop saying that." I nudged her.

"Not just any guy would fix a car for free and detail the

inside for no reason. Unless there is a reason, and that reason is that he likes you," Aerie practically purred.

"The reason is that Wyatt Holland is just a really nice guy." I put the car in reverse and stepped on the gas a little too hard.

"With dreamy eyes."

"Hello, you're dating Sam," I reminded her.

"I'm not interested in Wyatt. But you should be."

"Quit trying to marry me off. You'd think you didn't need me."

"I need you. You're not going anywhere." Aerie stopped joking. "I'd be destroyed if someone, well...destroyed the diner. Poor Heather."

The drive over to Spring Creek Plaza was miraculously smooth. I wondered what magic Wyatt performed on Babs. She hadn't driven this nicely in years.

When we arrived at the plaza, I parked the Buick in front of Pocket Moon Pottery. The decorated plate glass window was now completely gone. And Heather was struggling to tape paper across the window frame.

Aerie and I got out and helped Heather stretch the paper across the open space and tape it against the wall. Inside the shop, Heather had done an excellent job cleaning. Multiple black trash bags of broken pottery were stacked against the side wall. Other than that, the place was practically spotless. A few remaining pieces of pottery lingered on the shelves, looking lonely.

"You did a great job cleaning up," Aerie said.

"It was actually very therapeutic." Heather looked more upbeat. "It felt like I was cleaning out all of the negative and starting over. I even placed an order for new pottery. Something I had been wanting to do for a while."

"That's great. Is there anything else we can help you with?" I asked.

"I'd like to hear your thoughts on any of the suspects."

"We both feel that we should complete the interviews of all the women who were at the party the night of the murder."

We heard the crunch of car tires in the parking lot just outside the window. The door was pulled open with a flourish, and in stepped a woman wearing a bit more makeup than necessary. "I heard that Vicki Hudson was killed here at the studio. Is that true?"

Aerie and I stared at the woman hoping she'd introduce herself. But it appeared that Heather already knew her. "She was. Are you here to gloat or something?"

"Not at all! It's such a horrible thing to have happen in one's own studio. But I'm not surprised about Vicki."

I couldn't pass that lead up. "Why aren't you surprised?"

"She was an adulterer. Cheaters are bound to find a dastardly end one way or another."

"How do you know?"

"Oh, one hears things. You know, through the grapevine. It is a shame that it had to happen *here*. I bet your business will take a pretty bad hit."

"Don't worry about my business, Crystal. I can get it back on track."

"Oh, I'm sure you will. I'm sure you will." She nodded with a tiny grin on her face.

I could tell Aerie was thinking the same thing I was and hoping this woman would simply leave. Heather had already been through enough; there was no need for someone to meanly recap it all. But Crystal looked like she was just winding up. I wondered if she knew more about the murder. She took a few steps deeper into the studio and glanced around the room. "You cleaned up everything well. Heard the husband bashed everything into pulp. Such a shame. I hope you have insurance."

"I do and you'll be glad to know they've already given me an estimate."

"Well, that's good. I wouldn't want to hear that this whole episode caused your business to go under."

"Then, Crystal, you would own the only pottery place in the county. Lonely but lucrative. Unfortunately, I have no plans on giving up. So, you can go back to your own studio and help your own customers and don't worry a thing about me."

The beep-beep-beep sound of a truck backing up made all of us jump. Especially Crystal. "Fine. I'm leaving." She yanked open the door and left.

A few seconds later a deliveryman came in carrying a large box. "Hey Heather. I got some pottery."

"Thanks Brad." Heather signed for the package and Brad waved to us as he left.

Heather's mood lightened as she placed the box on the counter. "My new beginning. I paid for same-day-delivery so I wouldn't have to look at those empty shelves." She opened a pair of scissors and ran it along the packing tape.

"You handled Crystal very well," Aerie said admiringly.

"Crystal and I have had our run-ins over the years. I was expecting her to come by and gloat."

"I just added her to our suspect list."

Heather let out a half-laugh. "Crystal? She's petty but she wouldn't kill anybody."

Aerie and I looked at each other. If we learned anything over the past few months, it was that everyone was a suspect.

7

———

When I opened the door to my house there were equal amounts of purring and rubbing and jumping and licking from my resident animal friends. A huge squawk came from the corner of the dining room. "Welcome to the cantina. Welcome to the cantina."

"Hey, Taco, how's it going?"

Taco squawked again, a sound that reverberated throughout the room. I felt Arnold tense under my hand as I petted his head. I squatted next to him. "Guess what I have for you."

You smell like kitty treats.

"Yes, and I also got you something to snuggle with. Something that's just for you." I showed him the cat bed. Arnold hopped on top and kneaded it with his paws.

Can I have the treats, please.

"Single-minded as always. Yes, you can have the kitty treats while we take Ozzie for a walk."

The heat radiated off the sidewalk as Aerie and I took Ozzie out. The air had only cooled a bit once the sun went down. "Do you think it will rain?" I looked up at the puffy white clouds overhead.

"We could use it to break up this heatwave." Aerie held Ozzie's leash and stopped at a tree to let her sniff around. "We've learned that Tayla and Vicki obviously had some shared anger issues."

"That's for sure. I wonder why, though. No one seems to want to share the details." I put question marks in the notebook I brought along. We looped around the neighborhood as the late evening turned to night and when we turned back down Market Street, there was someone standing at my front door.

"What is she doing here?" Aerie's hackles were raised.

"I suppose it makes it easier for us to interview her about the party." I shrugged.

"Can I sneak out the back?"

"The back of where? She's going to see you in about ten seconds."

Ozzie barked. "Traitor," Aerie grumbled.

Chelsea turned around and saw us. She looked like someone had just put lemon juice in her Sugar Pops. But then whenever she was around Aerie and me, she was sour and irritated. Come to think of it, so were we.

"Do either of you know where Jay is? He's not answering his phone."

Aerie pulled out her phone and dialed Jay. It was obvious he picked up on the first ring. "Oh, nothing, I butt dialed. Sorry." She stuffed her phone back in her pocket, and didn't even try to hide her grin.

Chelsea's shoulders slumped defeated. "He's avoiding me."

Chelsea looked so dejected, I almost felt bad for her. "Why don't you come inside for a little bit." I put the key in my door and pushed it open. Shockingly, Chelsea quietly followed us inside.

"I need to set up the fans. It got hot in here fast." Aerie made her way into the living room and I headed to the kitchen. I examined the window closely before putting the fan in. The cool night air washed over me as I stood enjoying the breeze. I let my eyes close. The next thing I knew, the fan was falling out of the window as it slammed shut.

"What was that?" Chelsea shouted.

I took a deep breath. "It's my resident ghost."

"You two are crazy," she said without enthusiasm.

"You're still welcome to stay for a soda," I called to her as I propped the fan back into the window. When I walked out to the dining room, I was surprised to find Chelsea slumped in the folding chair with her head down on the table.

I placed the can of soda next to her. Aerie and I exchanged looks.

"I think I've messed it up," Chelsea whispered into the table. She took a deep breath and leaned back into the chair and noticed the soda. She picked it up and opened it. "You don't have any ice?"

"No." The appliances might have been paid for, but they weren't yet delivered. I still didn't have a decent refrigerator and the freezer section of the dorm fridge I did have was full of ice pops. After a few moments of awkward silence, I got up the courage. "Do you want to talk about it?"

Chelsea looked between me and Aerie. "With you guys?" She puffed out air. "No." She said it like I had made the most absurd suggestion ever.

"Okay, then." I exchanged glances again with Aerie. "Why are you here?"

"Besides looking for Jay, I figured you two are going to be

up to your eyeballs in this new murder mystery." She said it with all the snark imaginable. "And I knew the two of you would want to talk to me. So, I figured I would make your lives easier."

"Yay, for us," Aerie added, her voice flat. She had her own quirky defensive attitude when it came to Chelsea.

I wasn't going to look a gift horse in the mouth, even if it was Chelsea. "Okay, tell us what happened."

"It was nothing. That crazy Vicki got all out of whack about it, and yelled at Tayla for no reason, and when Tayla defended herself, Vicki threw her platter to the floor and it smashed everywhere."

"We heard that Tayla did it on purpose and that she was the one who started the fight."

"Whoever told you that was seeing things. It was all Vicki; she was acting weird during the entire party and then it was like she lost her mind or something. I just feel bad for Tayla, she has it bad enough."

"What do you mean she has it bad?"

"I'm not airing any dirty laundry with the two of you." Chelsea took a long sip of her soda.

"It sounds like Tayla has motive for murder."

"Hardly. She was hanging out with me after the party broke up."

"What were you doing?"

"Complaining about men." Chelsea glanced briefly at Aerie. "Look, I gotta go." She glanced around the room and made a face. "You two are cramping my style like in a big way." Chelsea pushed away from the table and got up to leave.

Aerie stood. "Do you want me to let Jay know you're looking for him?"

"No, if he wants to stay out all night again, that's his

business. I don't care." She realized she had shared more than she wanted and grimaced. "I'm leaving." She pushed her way out of the house and let the screen door slam shut.

"What was that all about?"

I shrugged.

"I am definitely going to work on setting you up...Jay might be available soon."

"Don't, Aerie. Leave Jay alone. Promise?" He was obviously working something out with Chelsea and I didn't want to be in the middle of it. "Are you up for interviewing Tayla tomorrow?"

Chelsea's story had only served to muddle what we thought had happened at the BYOB girls pottery night. We needed to find out what had really happened.

"Absolutely."

TAYLA WAS a teacher's aide at the day care and summer camp that was held at the elementary school. We would have to wait until after three o'clock to meet with her. Which worked around our diner schedule for a Monday.

After yoga class, we opened the diner, and moments later Mrs. Orsa joined us for breakfast. "I've been craving one of those strawberry muffins since I had one yesterday. I do hope there's more left?"

"Of course, I made extra." Aerie winked at Mrs. Orsa. I smiled. She was one of our dearest customers. I remembered what Heather had said about Vicki being one of her best customers. If someone hurt Mrs. Orsa at our diner, that would feel extremely personal to me. I imagined Heather felt the same way.

Dan came into the diner soon after. "Hey Aerie, how has your morning been?"

"Good, what can I get you?"

"Breakfast sandwich and one of your brown sugar oat shakes."

"Ah, I converted you over to the vegan side."

"You did." He grinned at Aerie and glanced at me quickly. "I can't stay, I'm still working the case. Can I get everything to go?"

"Sure, just hang out here and we'll put it together for you."

I went back into the kitchen wondering if things between Dan and me would get back to our usual mutual antagonism any time soon. These days everything was just awkward and weird.

I put the sausage patty on the grill and set the bun on the warm section to toast.

Aerie popped into the kitchen, excited. She grabbed a piece of chalk, put two more breakfast sandwiches on the board, and spun around to face me.

"All your men are here."

"What are you talking about?"

"Wyatt and Jay just showed up."

I shook my head. "You're being ridiculous."

"Dan's feathers are all ruffled. I think he's jealous of Wyatt's attention."

"Again. Ridiculous." I flipped the sausage and added two more. Aerie sure could make up stories to fit her narrative. Sheesh.

The bells on the door chimed again and Aerie dashed out.

I heard her shouting now, obviously for my benefit. "Hi

Brad, of course we can get you a breakfast sandwich and coffee."

I had to glance out into the dining room. Aerie managed to pique my interest. I had no idea who Brad was. Once I saw the brown uniform, I shook my head. The delivery guy was not interested in me in the least. But then he saw me and winked.

"Good grief," I said under my breath. I went back to the grill. "I'm staying right here until the end of the day." I put another sausage patty on the grill.

After wrapping the sandwiches, I put them in the pass-thru for Aerie to pick up.

"You're missing all the testosterone out here," she whispered.

"Ha, that's fine. I'll stay in the kitchen where you can't set me up."

She frowned at me and took the sandwiches.

Wyatt was the only one that came in at lunchtime. Dan sent Tyler Stewart in to pick up his lunch. We didn't see Jay or the delivery guy. That was probably for the best.

This time it was burgers all around. These guys liked to make my job easy. Mostly. I went out to greet Wyatt while the burgers sizzled just to quickly thank him again for leaving the car for me. Tyler had his back to me, staring at his phone while he waited for his order.

"Hey, Wyatt. Thanks again for leaving my car."

"How's she running?"

"Like a dream. Whatever magic you performed, she's running even better than her old self."

"Good to hear. If you have any problems just bring her by."

"Sure thing. How is your day going?"

"I only have a buffing and a paint job to do today. Someone keyed a driver side door."

At that Tyler turned and focused on Wyatt. "Whose car are you working on?"

"No offense, officer, but I don't like to share my client's personal situations. But if you need to know, you can come down to the shop, I'm sure my cousin will talk to you."

"Just making conversation." Tyler went back to his phone.

Wyatt shifted his attention in my direction. "Could I get fries with the burger?"

"Sure. I'll go drop them in the fryer." I was more than happy to leave the boys to themselves while I cooked.

Once the burgers were done and wrapped, and Tyler had left, I brought Wyatt his fries. "What was that all about not sharing client's information?"

"To tell you the truth, it's not really a big deal. But I didn't want to get Kurt in any more trouble than he's already in."

"Kurt got his car keyed?"

"Yeah, I guess someone thinks he was responsible for Vicki's death or something. Who knows? It's not for me to say. And I didn't want the officer to jump to conclusions, so I kept it to myself."

Aerie leaned over. "I wonder who would key Kurt's car."

Wyatt cleared his throat. "Now don't you start jumping to any conclusions."

Aerie waved them off. "Mira and I are like private investigators. We take in all the information and come up with the truth."

"We are not private investigators."

"It has a nice ring to it though, doesn't it?" She grinned.

"It implies we know what we're doing."

"Good point." Aerie nodded sagely. "Most of the time we don't know what we're doing. But it does all come out in the end."

"I'll clean up the kitchen so we can talk to Tayla. Thanks again, Wyatt."

"Thanks for the great meal, both of you. See you all later."

"Why is it so easy for you to talk to Wyatt but not Dan or Jay?"

"Because Wyatt... I think of Wyatt as more of a big brother."

"Well, if I wasn't with Sam, Wyatt wouldn't be my big brother."

"If Sam could hear you..." I shook my finger at her.

"I'm just teasing. Sam is all I need."

"That's good. Because you guys are too cute for words."

"Speaking of words, let's go have a few with Tayla. Then maybe we can head over to Sam's for dinner. He put some picnic tables with umbrellas out front. We can sit where it's cooler."

EVEN THOUGH THE weather was sunny and hot, Aerie and I decided to walk to the elementary school. Neither of us could stomach the idea of getting into one of our hot cars that had been baking in the August sun all morning.

By the time we got up to the building, the camp day had ended. Parents were picking up kids and groups were walking home. Once the chaos cleared, teachers started calling it a day and exiting the building. Thankfully, we didn't have to wait in the sun too long. Tayla came out and headed toward the parking lot.

"Tayla? Can we talk with you for a quick second?" I asked. She looked at both of us, curious.

"We'll only be a minute. We promise," Aerie said.

Tayla glanced up at the sun and rested her hand on her stomach. "You mind if we sit in the shade? It's a little too hot out here."

"Sure, lead the way." We followed her around the corner of the school to a pair of picnic benches under a large chestnut tree. Tayla set her purse down on the table along with her binder.

"You want to know about the fight I had with Vicki the night she died." It wasn't a question. She knew why we were here.

"I already talked to Detective Lockhart."

"We're helping Heather find closure."

Tayla gave us an amused look. "I know you guys help solve all the murders. It's not a big secret."

"Can you tell us more about what happened at the party?"

"Sure. Vicki and I have had this ongoing argument over a dress of mine that she had borrowed."

"A dress?" This was the first time we were hearing about a dress.

"It was a very expensive dress that I had bought recently when I went into the city. She spilled wine on it. And refused to pay for the dry cleaning."

"The two of you were fighting over this the night of the party?" None of the witnesses mentioned anything about a dress.

"That's the reason we fought. That night she also accused me of spilling paint on her stupid pottery."

"Did you?"

"Yes."

Both of us stared at Tayla for a moment. She replied, "She owes me like a hundred bucks. Well, she did. I guess I'm never getting it now."

"I suppose we are now speculating if you would kill her over a hundred dollars," I said. Sometimes the direct approach worked wonders. But then Tayla stood. "Look guys, it's hot, and I'm not feeling well." She rested her hand on her stomach. "I need to get home where it's cooler."

I pulled my legs out from under the picnic table and stood. Aerie joined me. The interview wasn't as productive as I hoped.

"Is there anything else you want to tell us?"

Tayla tightened up. "No." She said it a little too hastily.

I nodded. Just knowing she was still hiding something made this interview worth it.

"We'll let you get home."

"Have a good day, Tayla," Aerie added as we watched her head toward her car.

Aerie turned to me once we knew Tayla was out of hearing range. "She's hiding something."

"Definitely."

"We could go talk to her brother."

"Officer Stewart? I don't know if that's a good idea. Then Dan will know we're horning in on his business." I said.

"Please. He knows we'd be doing this anyway. I'm surprised we haven't bumped into him already on the investigative trail. We might as well follow our leads."

I put my hand on my hip. "Do you really think that Tyler will talk to us? I have a feeling his loyalties are with Dan and not the two of us."

"You might be right, but if his little sister is looking like a suspect, my guess is Tyler would want to help her out."

"Aren't they twins?" I asked.

"Yep, but I think he considers himself older. A first-out-of-the-womb twin thing."

I shook my head. Something was definitely going on with Tayla, we just didn't know what. If we had to talk to her brother to find out, we would do it. "Let's head over to the plaza where we can grab some dinner and you can chat with Sam. I want to stop by and see if Heather is at her shop."

"Why? Do you want to check on her to see how she's doing?"

"Yes, but also to see if she knows anything more about Tayla," I said.

"Good idea."

"Visiting Sam? Or chatting with Heather?"

"Both." Aerie grinned.

OUR QUICK CHAT with Heather didn't net much information. She didn't know Tayla very well or what her current situation was. But Sam's pizza was as good as always. And Aerie and Sam remained as cute as ever.

I dropped off Aerie at her house and headed home. I needed to mull over what we knew. Maybe I just needed some snuggle time with Arnold.

When I got home, I gave Arnold some placating treats, then I took Ozzie out for a long walk. Once the sun set, the air cooled enough that it was bearable. I still felt the heat rising off the sidewalk, but Ozzie didn't seem to mind. She was thrilled to be out of the stuffy house. Even the long walk didn't clear my mind of the realization that we weren't getting anywhere with our investigation. Maybe it was time to talk to the women at the newspaper. Their job was reporting after all. They should be in the know.

I brought Ozzie back inside and hung up her leash. She bounded over to her water dish and lapped up in messy gulps as much water as she could hold.

Really. Cats are so much neater with their water than dogs.

"How's your day going, Arnold?"

I wish it were cooler. These summer days are much too uncomfortable to nap for very long. It's almost driving me to want to sleep under the house like a common animal. But, I resist.

"Well, I appreciate it because you would have to get a bath afterward and that would not be fun.

It would never happen.

I gave him a look.

When will you come back with my kittens?

You want the kittens?"

They're my offspring. Why would I not want them?

"They're currently with their mom. She needs to feed them for at least six weeks, and I can't keep kittens here."

Why not? You keep Ozzie, you keep Ta-co. He drew out the word Taco in such a way to let me know just how much the bird irritated him.

"For now, they have to stay with their mother. A mother cat has to take care of babies until they are ready to leave." And before I could argue the point that we didn't need more animals in the house, a thought struck me. Chelsea mentioned that Tayla had problems, big problems. And when we had interviewed her, she rested her hand on her abdomen, twice, and she mentioned she wasn't feeling well. Granted, the hot sun can make anyone feel less than optimal, but if my theory was true, that might explain a number of things. Maybe the women at the newspaper would know.

I texted Aerie. *I have an idea. Let's head to the Pleasant Pond Independent after we close tomorrow.*

Sure thing. Have a good night.

With this new potential lead, I was feeling a little bit better about the investigation. "Come on Arnold, let's go to bed."

If you think I'm going to snuggle with you in this heat. You have another thing coming.

8

After we closed up the diner for the day, Aerie and I headed to the Pleasant Pond Independent newspaper office in the basement of the community center next to the church.

On the walk over, I shared my theory that Tayla might be pregnant.

Aerie stopped in her tracks. "Do you think so?"

"I don't really know. I just get that vibe. Things that she did yesterday and how she behaved, but I know it's just a thought. Maybe some of the women at the newspaper might have an inside scoop on the latest gossip."

"We can ask." She continued walking.

When we arrived, we found everyone outside at the picnic tables celebrating a birthday.

"You guys are just in time to have some of my cake." It appeared that Mia, wearing a Happy Birthday tiara, had just turned twenty-five. "Come, sit down."

A gentle breeze wafted through the shade under the trees. Even though the day was still hot, it was a pleasant place to hold the party. We accepted our slices of cake. I was more than happy to dig into mine. It had been a busy afternoon at the diner, and I had forgotten to eat lunch.

I quickly polished off the cake and glanced at the women sitting around the two picnic tables. Most of the women here had been at the party the other night. Josie, Mia, Sophia, and Gloria had been there. Amelia and Malinda, the editor, had not.

"Thanks for the cake. We can ask questions later. We don't want to ruin Mia's birthday party talking about Vicki's murder," Aerie said.

Mia waved a hand. "It won't ruin anything. Hopefully we can help. We have been talking about it all day trying to figure out who did it."

"Does anybody have any ideas?" I asked.

Gloria, who enjoyed offering sage advice, sat up straight. "After seeing what Vicki's husband, Kurt, did to the pottery shop, Sophia and I believe he might have done it. Maybe in some kind of violent rage or something."

"Does anyone know if they were having any marital problems?" I scanned the women's faces, trying to determine if their expressions might give anything away.

"Not any different from anyone else. I knew they had their fights. But I wasn't very close to Vicki."

"Does anyone know who *was* close to her?"

"I think she kept to herself most of the time. Although she and Tayla were pretty tight friends. But then they have a history."

"That's why I think Tayla did it. There's always been some kind of drama between the two of them for as long as I can remember. There was this time in high school..." Mia turned to Josie. "Remember when Tayla stole Vicki's boyfriend?"

Josie nodded. "But it's possible it could have been Tyler."

"Her twin brother? He's a cop," Gloria said.

"He always had a thing for Vicki, maybe he got jealous or...oh, maybe they were having an affair?" Mia said.

"Who was having an affair?" Sophia asked.

"Tyler," Mia repeated.

"That would be another reason for Kurt to be the murderer," Sophia added.

Josie shook her head. "Then Kurt would have killed Tyler."

"I don't think it's Kurt. He's a very nice young man," Gloria said.

"Then how do you explain the rage event at the pottery shop?" Mia said.

"A dead wife." Gloria said.

"I still think it's the person you least expect. It's Tayla, for sure," Josie said.

"What if it was both Tayla and Tyler?" Mia lit up at the prospect of double murderers.

"Okay, now you're just being crazy," Josie reprimanded.

I glanced over at Aerie. Things were spiraling out of control with the allegations. But I continued to take mental notes. We might have to talk with Tayla again after all.

Malinda cleared her throat. "I think you're forgetting about one of the most important aspects of this mystery." We turned to the paper's editor. "Vicki's father is a lawyer in the city. You never know what kind of intrigue that might cause."

"Do you think Vicki's father may have angered the wrong person?" I asked.

"It's a possibility that can't be dismissed," Malinda added.

I turned to Malinda. "Do you know what kind of law he practices?"

She swallowed her forkful of cake. "Criminal defense."

Aerie and I exchanged another glance. This was definitely something we needed to look into.

"Malinda, do you know of any criminals that might have a vendetta against Vicki's father?"

"As a matter fact, I remember something a few years ago. We published a short article on it. I can go through the archives and find it for you." She took out her phone and made a note.

"That would be wonderful. Thanks," Aerie said.

I knew we needed to continue the questioning. We might not get a chance to have everyone together again. "For those of you that were at the party, did you hear anything out of the ordinary?"

"You mean besides the fight between Vicki and Tayla?" Josie asked.

Aerie nodded. "Was anything else different, anything odd or strange?"

Gloria leaned forward. "Personally, I thought it was odd that Heather waited so long before she tried to break up the fight between Vicki and Tayla. All of us knew it was just going downhill and getting worse."

"Then Vicki threw the platter."

"I thought Tayla threw the platter?"

"No. I am pretty sure it was Vicki. She said Tayla ruined her artwork and now it was useless, and she threw it."

Gloria shook her finger. "You know? I remember the side door being open. Because it was so hot in the pottery room with the kiln going in the back."

"No, I thought Tayla threw it. She grabbed it from Vicki and threw it."

I paused. "Wait, Gloria, you saw an open back door?"

"That could allow anyone to come inside."

"Especially if Heather might have forgotten to close it, or maybe even lock it for the night?"

"Thank you for the cake, and all the information." Aerie said.

"Especially the information. We now have more to go on than we did before." That was for sure. We had a number of new leads. Although I didn't think all of them would go anywhere, it was still better to have too many than not enough.

We left the newspaper crew to argue over who they thought made the best suspect for Vicki's murder. We now had a laundry list of leads to check out. I wanted to ask Heather if there was a possibility she could have left the back door open the night of the murder. And I hoped Malinda would be able to find the article she had referenced about Vicki's father.

"I can try to talk to Tyler," Aerie said.

I turned toward her. "You want to interview him?"

"Sure. I babysat them once when I was a teenager. I might be able to find out if he knows anything about Tayla's situation, and what the fight was really about."

"If you think you can find out more, let's go for it."

ON OUR WAY back to the house we stopped by the diner. I made Aerie and myself sandwiches and we brought them back to my house. Jay's black pickup truck was parked out front.

"Jay said he would bring by the cabinets this afternoon. I gave him your spare key. I hope you don't mind," Aerie said.

"He has the cabinets, already?" I lengthened my stride to pick up the pace.

"You're super excited to get your kitchen back, aren't you?" Aerie huffed out.

"No offense, but cooking everything in an insta-pot or at the diner is getting a little bit old." I was practically running now.

"You can't really cook anything with the cabinets. You know that, right?" Aerie called out behind me.

"Obviously. But it's one step closer to an actual kitchen!" I pushed the key in the lock and it stuck; one of the hazards of old houses, old locks, but by the time I had the door unlocked, Aerie was by my side.

When I finally opened the front door, we were heralded by an extremely loud Taco screeching. Ozzie jumped at our knees and Arnold sat aloof, regarding everything with a level of smugness that only Arnold could achieve.

"Hey, guys." I scratched Ozzie behind the ears and petted Arnold quickly.

"Go ahead, I know you want to see the cabinets and talk to Jay. I can take Ozzie for a quick walk." Aerie grabbed Ozzie's leash and clipped it to her collar.

"Thanks." I walked over to say hi to Taco so he would stop his screeching. My ears were ringing. Taco finally settled down.

"Hey, Mira. The cabinets are almost done."

I had been expecting some basic cabinetry. But what I saw was Jay finishing the installation of some beautiful, beveled dove gray cabinets.

"Oh," I exclaimed.

"You don't like them?" Jay sounded concerned.

"No, no. They're gorgeous." I walked to the nearest one and gently touched my dream cabinet. "When you said you were demo-ing, I expected something that looked more, well...leftover."

"They came from a house that was upgrading their kitchen. I put word out that I was looking for cabinets. One of my buddies a couple towns over came across them and was careful taking them out."

"Thank you so much. And thank your friend." I marveled at all the cabinet space I would now have. It was beginning to look like a real kitchen.

"I talked to Bob over at the hardware store. He says your appliances should be in soon. I can bring a couple guys over and we can install them for you pretty quickly. Just let us know when they show up."

"Jay, this is marvelous. Thank you." I was grinning so much my cheeks hurt.

"All the hard work was worth it, getting to see that smile."

I felt my cheeks heat in a blush.

Jay coughed to cover the nervous silence. "Well, I'm done here. Enjoy the kitchen. I'll see you later when the appliances arrive." He headed out the back door of the kitchen.

I walked the perimeter of the kitchen with nervous energy. I took a deep gulp of air. "Well, that was awkward," I said under my breath. I turned back toward the doorway to see Jay stepping back into the kitchen holding out my spare keys. "I suppose you want to give these back to Aerie."

"Oh, yeah, thanks."

He gently laid the keys in my hand. I felt the warm brush of his fingers against mine. A shiver went down my back. Just then, the fan fell out of the window, which slammed shut, making us both jump. I inadvertently took a step toward Jay, and he stepped toward me. We were practically in each other's arms. My eyes met his.

"Are you okay?" he asked. "I really should see about fixing this window." He walked purposefully past me.

"I thought you said there wasn't anything wrong with it."

"Obviously there's something wrong with it. A window shouldn't fall shut like this. I'll bring over a new window later this week. I'll swap it out."

"Okay. If you think that'll work."

"Now I really need to be going."

I nodded. Jay exited the kitchen door once more and the tension slowly left the room.

"Hey." Aerie had come back with Ozzie. "Oh, pretty. Did Jay just leave?"

"What? Yeah."

"What's up with you?"

To recover from that moment with Jay, I took a deep breath. "I'm just surprised at how pretty the cabinets turned out."

"Yeah, Jay has a great network of contractor friends. He can find anything."

I secretly wondered if he had specifically asked for upscale cabinets. But I pushed that thought out of my mind. "Come on, let's eat our sandwiches and put a list together."

"We got a lot of information from the women at the newspaper yesterday. My head is still spinning." Aerie walked back out into the dining room. We sat at the table and dug into the sandwiches. Turkey, bacon, Swiss on whole wheat was a pretty good combination. Arnold hopped up and landed in the center of the table.

Don't I get anything to eat? A treat perhaps.

"Sorry Arnold, did you want something?"

The fact that I have to ask is an insult.

"Let me get you some treats to remedy that." I still hadn't told Aerie that I could hear Arnold's thoughts. Since it was just run-of-the-mill to talk to our furry friends, I could cover up my 'gift' easily. I gave Arnold a big handful of treats to keep him busy and I went back to my sandwich. I glanced at the box that Darla had sent making a mental note to open it and deal with whatever was inside. But not right now. Right now, we had to make our suspect list.

"I think we need to look at Tayla."

I nodded. I wrote her name at the top of the page. "And the fact she might be pregnant." I added that next to her name.

"Definitely put Kurt's name up there at the top. And we should talk to Tyler just to see if we could get more information about his sister."

"I agree. And don't forget he might be a suspect as well. Although, after meeting him, I would find it really hard to believe." I wrote down Tyler's name.

"Even if Tyler appears innocent, we've learned everyone goes on the list," Aerie reminded me.

"And let's not forget about Vicki's father and anyone he might have come across."

"I think he lives in the city. I'm not sure how we would get a hold of him. Vicki doesn't have any siblings where I could get information."

"What about her mother?"

"I think her mother's been out of the picture since she was little. I only remember her living with her father."

I nodded and crossed off "mother" from the list.

"Well, this is the longest list we've ever had. Plus, I suppose anyone could have been angry at a lawyer, angry with Vicki's father, so we don't even know all the possible suspects." I wrote down *Someone angry @ V's lawyer father*. "It could be anybody. This list is open-ended."

"We also need to talk to Heather again about the

possibility that the back door was open the night of the murder."

"You're right. I forgot about that." I wrote down, *Open door?*

"We can text Heather, right now." Aerie picked up her phone and thumbed a message.

"Let me know when she responds and I'll add that info to the list."

"Now we have a good list to work from. I'm going to head home. Thanks for making the sandwiches." Aerie got up, and immediately bent to give Arnold a goodbye pat. He was licking his paws under the table, and stopped momentarily to acknowledge the love.

"No problem. Thanks for having a diner." I grinned.

"Don't worry, your kitchen is coming together. You will be cooking in there before you know it."

I smiled wider and nodded. She was right. Just a little bit longer and I would have my own working kitchen. With amazing high-end cabinets. "Okay, I'll see you at yoga tomorrow morning."

"Bye, Taco." Aerie waved to the big scarlet macaw in the corner. Taco moved back and forth along his perch. "She's a hottie, she's a hottie."

"Snarky bird." Aerie shook her head and headed out the door.

9

____

The next morning, Arnold was kind enough to wake me up at the crack of dawn so he could get more treats and a can of cat food.

"You know if you waited another fifteen minutes my alarm would go off."

My alarm is my stomach. When it says it's hungry, it's time to eat.

I let out a huge yawn, slowly got dressed, and fed the animals. I was still yawning while taking Ozzie up the street and back for her morning walk.

When I returned, Arnold wanted a refresh of his water dish. As I set down the water, I addressed my overly spoilt cat. "Thanks to you I have time to spare this morning and can get to Aerie's yoga class early."

You're welcome.

The morning air was cool and refreshing, and I took my time walking up to the rec center at the church. When I arrived, Aerie was still setting up and I helped her with the yoga props in the mats.

"Good morning," Aerie cheerfully greeted Sophia from

the newspaper. She was also obviously a morning person, unlike me. I stifled another yawn. Sophia looked around making sure we were still the only people in the room, and kept her eye on the door, while she edged close to Aerie and me. "Can I talk to the two of you after class today?"

"Sure," Aerie said.

I nodded, stifling another yawn. But the look of concern on her face acted like caffeine to my system. What did she have to tell us?

Mrs. Orsa came in, and we broke up our chat.

It was a challenge to stay focused during class. I ran through every possible reason that Sophia could have more information than what she shared with us yesterday during the birthday party. Shutting down my mind during yoga— or anytime—was not a skill in my arsenal. By the end of class, I had come to three realizations: Either she knew something yesterday and didn't want to share it in front of all the other women, she was going to implicate someone in the yoga room, or she had recently seen or heard something. Either way, by the end of class I was a ball of nerves wondering what she was about to share. Not the state of mind Aerie preferred her clients in at the end of a yoga class.

Aerie was by far more patient than I was in saying her goodbyes to the students. Thankfully, Sophia hung back and waited until the last person left.

"I didn't want to say anything yesterday because then I would never hear the end of it. Everyone would be asking me questions for more details, and I only saw what I saw."

"What did you see?"

"I was over at the pond's parking lot. I was getting ready to leave. Probably around 7:30 p.m. When I walked over to my car, I noticed Tayla talking to someone through the window of a car. I couldn't see the person in the car—they were in shadows. Tayla was trying to keep it quiet, but she was really angry."

"Did you hear anything she said?"

"I was afraid to get any closer or she would notice me. I couldn't see who she was talking to. I didn't recognize the car. The only thing I heard was, "It's your fault.""

"You have no idea who was in the car? Was it a man or a woman?"

Sophia shook her head. "I really don't know. But Tayla took her car keys and dug them into the side of the driver's door and scratched enough paint off that I could see the damage from across the parking lot."

Aerie turned toward me. "That means we should be able to find the car if they live in town."

I immediately thought about what Wyatt said about having to do some bodywork on a car the other day. That it was Vicki's husband's car. Every investigative lead seemed to lean toward Kurt.

Aerie noticed my pondering look, thanked Sophia profusely, and walked her to the door. When she came back, she asked, "You know something, don't you?"

"Maybe. Wyatt said something at the diner the other day, but I'll need to check with him to see if it's who I think it is. What are the odds that more than one person got their car keyed last week?"

"Why? Who do you think it is?"

"Kurt Hudson."

"Oh, the plot thickens."

"Let's get back to the diner and start our workday so we can end it. Then I can get in touch with Wyatt and find out if I'm correct."

"If you are, we should probably talk with Dan."

I knew she was right, but I really wasn't looking forward to talking with Dan about the case. "Every time I talk to him, we end up yelling at each other."

"That's because you push each other's buttons," Aerie said with glee. She locked the door to the community center behind us.

The sun was now up in full force and was easy to predict it was going to be another stifling day.

"I think I'm going to make more sorbet. What do you think about raspberry lime?"

"That sounds fantastic! How long will we have to wait? To eat it?" So much for Aerie's patient glow after yoga.

"I haven't made the base yet, but the ice cream machine is prepped at a low temperature and should be ready to create a masterpiece at a moment's notice."

"I could use some of that right now." Aerie pulled her ponytail and shook out her hair and smoothed it back into a high ponytail. "Maybe we can head to the pond later. I mean, after you talk to Wyatt."

"That would be great." Summer was almost at an end and I had yet to spend any quality time at the pond. The town was named for it after all. And nothing would feel better in this heat than a cool dip in the water.

But before any of that could happen, we needed to head to the diner for the breakfast rush, make some fruit sorbet, and eventually hunt down Wyatt to ask some very pointed questions.

BECAUSE OF OUR little chat with Sophia, we were late opening the diner. Mrs. Orsa stood out front, waiting in her usual spot. But someone else stood right behind her and I shook my head. I had been hoping that I wouldn't see him this morning. But Aerie was right. We had to tell Dan what we found out. Maybe he could shed some light on who was in the car. Maybe he already knew.

"Morning everyone." I kept my head down and unlocked the door.

"Sorry we're late this morning. Yoga ran over." I gave Aerie the side-eye. She never let yoga run over. She was like clockwork. I didn't bother to look at Dan. He probably knew that something was up. I walked briskly to the back of the diner. I didn't envy Aerie having to play it cool out front while I got to hide in the kitchen.

I turned on the grill and took everything out of the refrigerator that I needed to start breakfast. After a quick set-up, Aerie was back to write the orders on the chalkboard. Dan wanted his egg sandwich. Aerie had already taken care of Mrs. Orsa's breakfast muffin, but she came in the kitchen to microwave water for Mrs. Orsa's tea.

I started to grill the sausage patty and toast the English muffin while Aerie rushed to get the coffee pot started. We worked quickly. "You know we have to tell him."

"I know." I was resigned. "You do it."

"We'll both do it."

"Fine." When the sandwich was done and the coffee brewed, we took everything out to Dan Lockhart, detective extraordinaire. He sat at the counter absorbed in whatever he was reading on his phone. He glanced up when I placed the plate on the counter. Those eyes. My heart fluttered. I shook my head. I couldn't be crushing on Dan. We drove each other crazy.

"Thank you." He refolded his napkin and placed it next to his plate. He looked both of us in the eye. "Is there a reason the two of you are late opening the diner?"

This is how he made my blood boil. "We can't be late one morning?"

He tipped his head. "I know you two are up to something. Spill it."

"We don't have to tell you anything, Detective Lockhart. We're not suspects."

"Fine. You don't have to tell me anything." He smirked and picked up his breakfast and took a bite.

Aerie and I didn't move. We simply stared at him. What was this game he was playing? Did he know something? "Mmm. Good sandwich," he said with a lilt.

"You know we know something, don't you?" I asked, angry that the tables had turned.

"Nope," he said between bites.

Aerie beat me to it. "We talked with Sophia today after yoga and she says she saw Tayla Stewart having a very heated argument with someone in a car. At the end of the argument, she keyed the driver side door. Dramatically."

"Is that so?"

"So now, you tell us what you found out so far," I blurted.

Dan smiled slowly. "I don't discuss open investigations."

"What are you talking about? We just gave you a great piece of evidence."

"No, you didn't. You told me Tayla keyed someone's car."

"But she had an argument."

He nodded. "That usually comes before someone keys someone else's car."

"You're making fun of us."

"No. I'm not. But I still can't discuss open investigations." He took another bite of his sandwich and slowly chewed. After he swallowed, he continued, "You can let Heather know that I will continue to work on the case until it is solved."

"So will we," I said with as much snark as possible, and I marched back into the kitchen. I knew that meant that Aerie would have to smooth things over. I would just have to apologize to her later. Right now, I was fuming.

It was a slow morning at the diner and, because I didn't have anything else to occupy myself with, I went into the refrigerator and pulled out everything I needed to make raspberry lime sorbet.

I was probably a little rougher with the blender base and blender cup than I should have been. I fought with it until they clicked together. After rinsing the raspberries, I dropped them into the blender. I scrubbed the limes and used the microplane to zest them. I had a neat pile of bright green zest shavings when Aerie returned to the kitchen. Without looking up, I held out my hand. "Stop right there. I don't want to apologize to Dan. I don't want to hear anything more about him."

"Why are you so angry with him all of a sudden?"

"No reason." I wanted to turn back to the sorbet-making, but stopped myself. I had found that cooking angry made the food turn out less than optimal. That went with sorbet-ing as well. Creating in the kitchen was, for me, what yoga was for Aerie. I breathed deeply trying to channel zen-sorbet-ing-peace-of-mind.

"You like him and you realized it, finally." Aerie smelled the yummy zest and grinned.

"No. He drives me insane. I don't want to see his face ever again." I wiped my hands on my apron.

"That's because it's a good-looking face and he turns you on."

"You're crazy. Come over here and help me juice these limes."

I didn't have to look at Aerie to know she was still grinning from ear to ear. She took out the juicer with its yellow and green handles. "How much do you need?"

"One quarter cup."

She squeezed the limes into a measuring cup. "One of these days you have to start dating again."

"Well, I'm not going to be dating Dan." I shouted and then I realized that Dan might still be in the diner. My face heated up, probably turning raspberry red.

Aerie laughed out loud. "Don't worry, he left about five minutes ago."

"Don't scare me like that."

"You can start dating Dan again, you know. My brother is still delusional over Chelsea. Even if they are fighting right now."

"Yeah, I know. It's not like I'm waiting for your brother to become available, Aerie."

"What did he say to you?"

"Things he probably doesn't want his sister to know."

"You're kidding. What?"

"Don't worry, nothing important but I highly doubt he would appreciate if I told you." Normally Aerie and I didn't keep anything from each other, except that I could hear my cat speaking in actual words, in my mind, and, evidently when her brother shares his secrets.

"That's fine." Her voice went up an octave. "I'll find out myself." She squeezed the last lime exceptionally hard. "Here's your juice. The raspberries smell heavenly. And I'm probably going to kill Jay."

"He's not hiding anything from you."

"He better not be."

"If it was anything important, I would tell you."

"Promise?"

"Yes."

Aerie was now satisfied. Although honestly, I think Jay was in for a good argument when she found him. I suddenly pitied him. He was getting it from all sides lately.

"It's pretty slow this morning. If you want to go over to talk to Wyatt, I can hold down the diner."

"Yeah?" But I was in the middle of making the sorbet. "It can wait until after lunch. I want to finish this up first." I also was not in any mood to talk to Wyatt or to think about dating anyone anytime soon.

My frustration burned off as I blended up the raspberries and measured out and added the sugar. I poured the pureed mixture into the ice cream machine and soon I had a beautiful dark raspberry pink sorbet. I packed it in the round container we used for the freezer up front, and couldn't wait to share it with everyone. It didn't matter that Dan got on my nerves and refused to tell us anything. Aerie and I were fully capable of figuring things out on our own. And we had Heather's help too, this time around. We'd be just fine without Dan.

10

____

Customers began to come in for lunch while I was at the front freezer adding the raspberry lime sorbet to the canisters of ice cream already there. Aerie finished her decorative swirl on the "specials" chalkboard letting everyone know about the new sorbet.

I secretly hoped that Dan would forgo his daily lunch break at the diner. I couldn't handle that right now. I had just managed to calm myself down. As I turned to go back to the kitchen, the bells over the front door rang and I cringed thinking that it could be Dan, but Wyatt entered the dining room.

"I'm so glad it's you," I blurted out.

"I bet that's how you greet all your customers." Wyatt grinned and took a seat at the counter.

I blushed, embarrassed. "I just had a question to ask."

"Sure. What's up?"

I looked down at my hands, which were covered in raspberry juice and very sticky. "Let me wash up and I'll be right back."

"No problem. I'll order lunch."

I washed my hands quickly at the sink, but I realized Aerie was writing up a third order. I would need to cook lunch for everyone before I could talk to Wyatt. Besides, if the killer was who I thought it was, I wanted to be able to focus on Wyatt's reaction when I told him. I wanted to phrase my question to get the maximum amount of information from him.

I looked up at the board, memorized the orders, and worked around the kitchen cooking up everyone's lunch. I dropped fries in the fryer, threw hamburgers on the grill along with sliced onions. I toasted bread for a club sandwich and managed to plate all three orders in one go. I took a moment and smiled. I was getting the hang of this job as a short order cook. And I was pretty proud of it.

I put the plates on the counter of the pass-through and rang the little bell. Done. That's when Aerie came in with four more orders. No rest for the weary. I just hoped that Wyatt wouldn't leave before I was able to talk to him. I swung back into work mode and cooked up a storm. More burgers and fries, another club sandwich, and a fruit plate. The fruit plate took longer because I refused to precut any of the fruit. It always oxidized and was brown on the plate if I did it. I cut all the fruit when it was ordered. Finally, I plated the orders and had them ready for serving and walked out front while Aerie took the fruit to Gloria who was sitting in the back booth reading a novel. I was happy to find that Wyatt was still sitting at the counter his lunch long finished, reading something on his phone.

"You didn't have to wait for me. I could stop by after work."

"The garage is slow today I'm sure Jasper will be fine without me for a few more minutes. He said you had something to ask?"

"When I met you the other day, you had to do bodywork on a car." I watched Wyatt put up his guard.

"Kurt Hudson's was the only car that was keyed that you worked on, right?" I watched Wyatt's face closely for a response.

"You know I don't like to share client's information." Wyatt pinched his lips. "It's not good business."

"I understand. But it could help us figure out who killed Vicki."

"I highly doubt the fact that Kurt's car got keyed is evidence that he killed Vicki."

Glancing around at everyone eating their lunch, I whispered, "I didn't say that Kurt killed Vicki." Although, I was thinking it.

"I think you're reading too much into some poor guy getting his car keyed by an ex-girlfriend. And, yes, his was the only car brought in that was keyed. But that doesn't mean anything."

"Tayla is Kurt's ex-girlfriend?" That made things interesting. "Wait a minute, how would you know if Kurt and Tayla were exes?" I was so used to everyone knowing everyone else in town that I had forgotten Wyatt was actually newer than I was.

"My cousin Jasper is one of the worst gossips in town, I think, next to Ellie at the bank. Just don't go jumping to conclusions with the bit of information I gave you."

So, it was confirmed. Tayla and Kurt had an argument where Tayla keyed his car. Wyatt didn't believe Kurt could be a suspect in Vicki's murder. Could that mean Tayla could be? I was left pondering that thought when Wyatt stood up. "Well, I have to head back. Like I said, don't jump to conclusions just because I had to work on the guy's car."

"In my book everyone is a suspect until proven otherwise."

"I don't know, Mira; I think it's a pretty scary world to live in. Not to trust anyone."

"Not at all. It helps me keep an eye out for clues."

"Do me a favor and be careful with all this investigating. It's a sad thing that happened to Vicki. I wouldn't want to see you come to any harm."

"Thanks, Wyatt, but don't worry, Aerie has my back. Right, Aerie?"

"What? Oh yeah, I got your back."

Wyatt shook his head and chuckled as he walked out of the diner.

I wound my way between the tables to Aerie. "Did you know about Kurt and Tayla?"

"What about them?"

"That they are exes?"

"Nope, contrary to common belief I do not know everyone's business. Although I suppose Ellie might."

"I'll clean up the kitchen and then I'll head over to the bank."

"I'm coming too. A girl needs a little excitement. Plus, I just told Wyatt I had your back. Afterward, we can go over and visit Heather and give her an update."

"And visit Sam, of course."

"Of course."

I PULLED open the door to the bank's vestibule. A gush of highly air-conditioned air wafted out. I almost shivered. But it felt great to get out of the heat. Aerie sighed. "We should visit here more often."

"Hey Ellie, how's it going?"

"Hey, guys." Ellie perked up when she saw us. "How are you doing?"

"It's been busy at the diner." A quick glance around the bank showed that no one was around to overhear anything we said. "Hey Ellie, we need to find out what you know about Kurt Hudson and Tayla Stewart."

"Whoa, that's a juicy one. It's actually one of my favorites."

"Favorite what?"

"Favorite star-crossed lover triangles."

"Okay, spill it."

"Gladly." Ellie leaned forward on the stool behind the counter. "They say it started in middle school."

"There was a love triangle in middle school?"

"No, no. That's when Tayla and Vicki first met."

"Okay. Go on."

"Supposedly, one of them was getting picked on. The other came to her rescue. I can never remember which one, to tell you the truth. But anyway, they became fast friends. Super close, OG besties."

"Then what happened?"

"High school happened. Actually, not until their junior year, I think. But that's when Vicki met Kurt. Supposedly, they dated for a while and then broke up, and Kurt started dating Tayla. Vicki was all bent-out-of-shape because she figured Tayla would be on her side and not on Kurt's. Her best friend sided with her ex to the point where she was dating him? Lots of hurt feelings."

Aerie nodded. "I can imagine."

"Then what happened?" I asked.

"From what I heard, I don't think they dated for very

long. And when they broke up, Kurt immediately began dating Vicki again."

"Young love."

"I'm pretty sure that's why Tayla and Vicki barely talked to each other let alone tolerated each other."

"I see. That explains a lot." I shivered in the amazing air conditioning. "Do you know if Kurt and Tayla picked back up on their relationship?" It couldn't hurt to ask.

"I haven't heard anything in the local rumor mill, or online."

"There are online rumor mills?"

Ellie looked at Aerie like she was crazy. "Of course, that's the nexus of rumors and drama."

"Things are stacking up. We might have an idea who the killer is."

"My thought is that Tayla did it. I've met Kurt; he seems too nice. That Tayla, I don't know. She's a little too quiet. It makes me wonder just what's going on inside her head." Ellie sat back up on her stool. "But definitely let me know when you find out who it is. I'm dying to know."

"No problem. We'll keep you in the loop."

"I think we should talk to Dan."

"You can talk to Dan. I'm done with him," I told Aerie. I watched as she exchanged a look with Ellie that I didn't understand. "What? Why are you two looking like that?"

"No reason. I just think you have the hots for Dan and are afraid to believe it."

"What? No way. You guys are crazy." I headed toward the door.

"Aerie, you tell me when they get engaged." Ellie picked up a magazine and started reading.

I glared at Aerie. She just smiled. "Sure thing, Ellie. If I don't marry her off to my brother first."

Thankfully, the only thing that came out of Aerie's mouth on the walk back to the diner was a sappy grin.

"I'm not dating anybody. And that's final."

"That's what I said until I met Sam."

"Besides, didn't you just hear this love triangle story? One of them ended up dead."

Aerie's pace slowed for a second. "You do have three men all vying for your attention. But would that make a love quadrangle instead of a triangle?"

"I do not have three men," I firmly announced. "Arnold and Taco are enough for me."

"We'll see."

I shot her a dirty look. "Let's just go to the pizza pub and eat. The hunger pains are making me cranky at you."

"Fine, fine. I won't say anymore." But she was still grinning.

AERIE and I sat at a booth in Sam's pizza pub devouring a large vegan cheese pizza. Sam had added extra vegan cheese to our pie. Apparently, there wasn't as much demand for vegan cheese on pizzas this week. It was actually pretty good, so I didn't mind.

"Their prior relationship definitely makes things more interesting," I said.

"How so?" Aerie had a mouthful of pizza.

"Well, if Tayla really is pregnant and Kurt is the potential father, then it gives both of them reason to want Vicki out of the picture."

"Tayla's pregnant?" A deep voice sounded shocked directly behind me.

Aerie's eyes widened in surprise. I turned around in the booth and peered over the top to find officer Tyler Stewart glaring at the two of us. "Tayla is pregnant? How do you know?"

"Tyler, I'm so sorry. We're just going through our guesses around the suspect for Vicki's murder. It's just a guess."

"So, you just *think* she's pregnant? Why?"

"It's just a number of things we've noticed lately. I wouldn't worry about it. I'm sure you could just ask her." Boy was this embarrassing.

"I plan to." He flipped around and punched numbers into his phone.

I slid back into my seat wishing I could melt into it and disappear. I could tell by the look on Aerie's face she felt the same way.

"There's no answer." I heard officer Stewart on the other side of the booth. "I'm going to her house." A gust of hot air swept into the dining room as he left.

"We could be wrong," I shouted as the door dropped closed. Aerie and I were now in some very hot water.

Aerie gulped down her iced drink, then looked at me. "I don't think that could've gone any worse."

"I have to agree with you. Do you think he's going to hate me now?" The level of mortification made me nauseous. My big mouth landed us in trouble, yet again.

"No. But I can pretty much guarantee that Tayla will."

"Yeah." I gulped.

"I guess we won't be talking to her anytime soon," Aerie mumbled and then took a bite of her pizza.

"Probably not. But maybe we can get some information from Tyler."

"Do you think he would even consider talking to us at this point?"

"Maybe, I mean if we can tie Tayla back to a murder, we

can pretty much guarantee that Dan is not sharing any information with Officer Stewart.

"Good point. I suppose we should hope for the best. Now what?"

"We go looking for the other suspect."

"Kurt Hudson, the primary suspect? The guy that probably committed the murder?"

"Yeah, him. It'll be fine."

"With our track record I highly doubt it," she said. Then she smiled. "Bring Arnold. You told me he was like an attack cat."

"Ha, ha, I suppose we could find a public place to talk to him." I pondered our safety.

"See, now you're talking."

We settled our tab with Sam even though he didn't want us to pay. And we steeled ourselves to go back out into the heat and to talk with Kurt. Going on the hunt to speak with a potential killer had never been high on my to-do list. But it had to be done. I just wondered how bad of an idea this was. Maybe I should get over myself and tell Dan our ideas. On second thought, he could follow his own clues. We would follow ours, and find the killer first.

11

We went back to Aerie's house. I petted her kitty Snowball while she looked up the address for Kurt and Vicki Hudson.

"Got it."

"Where do they...I mean, where does he live?"

"Looks like it's not too far from the high school."

"We could walk." We still had no desire to get into a car steaming in the sun.

"We could, but it might be in our own best interest to have a getaway car nearby."

"Good point."

"Safety first." The jokes always came out when we were about to head into danger.

"Are you sure you don't want to bring Arnold?"

I shook my head. I never should've told her the story about the cat show. Although Arnold did show good use of his front and back claws, now that I thought about it. That guy didn't see it coming. "No. Let's just get this over with. A few choice questions and I should pick up a vibe on whether or not he's lying. How are your aura reading classes going?"

Aerie shrugged. "I don't know. I don't think I'm getting any better at it."

"Darla said you had talent. You just need to practice."

That made me think of the unopened box at my house. A wave of guilt ran through me. My sister was just being kind by sending something. I was the one who had a little-sister complex and wanted to live my own life, out from under her shadow. And as a famous psychic, that shadow was huge. But could I really fault that she just wanted to help her little sister? I vowed to open that box as soon as I got back home.

"I know. I guess I'm just second-guessing it."

"I'll ask the questions, you try to read his aura. Deal?"

"Deal."

"Either way we'll get some information out of him."

The two of us got in my car, and Babs started smoothly. Wyatt had worked some serious magic on this baby. I cranked the AC. And a blast of icy cold air came out. Much colder than it ever had been before. I'd have to thank him for that too. Because I'm pretty sure I hadn't had the AC charged in... forever. The drive up to Kurt's house took under two minutes. The house he lived in with Vicki was a tall Victorian a few streets over from the center of town. I parked on the street. We sat there and stared at the house. His car was in the driveway. By looking, I could tell that the car had just been washed. It looked shiny and new. You couldn't tell that Wyatt had repainted the driver side door. It was the same color as the rest of the car. For a fleeting moment as I looked at Babs' peeling gray paint I wondered if I should have Wyatt paint my old Buick. Who was I kidding? Peeling gray paint was part of her charm. "Isn't it, Babs?" I rubbed the dashboard.

"What?"

"Oh, nothing." I gave Babs a final pat. "Are you ready to go in?"

"Nope. You?"

"Me neither. Let's go." We opened our doors and left the air-conditioned oasis.

Our footsteps creaked on the front porch stairs as a stifling breeze blew through the porch. Without thinking about it too much, I knocked on the door.

We waited. I knocked again. And rang the doorbell. Twice.

"His car is in the driveway."

"But it's possible he's out. Somebody could have come by and picked him up, or he walked."

"Should we look around back?"

"Yeah. But I have a bad feeling about this."

"Yes, reminding me of Robbie's house. I don't know. It's giving me the shivers." Aerie shook her arms. "And it's too hot to have shivers."

We walked around the back of the house. I didn't notice anything out of the ordinary. The blinds weren't closed or anything.

Aerie knocked on the back door. "Mr. Hudson?" She shrugged.

"Wherever he is, he's not here."

"I think we should talk to Dan."

"Okay. Let's go." I felt resigned. "But you're going to do all the talking."

"Fine with me. Do you still have that feeling?" she asked me hesitantly.

"Yeah, that itchy kind-of, no-good feeling?"

"Yeah, that."

"I'll drive us to the police station. Let's get this over with." I wondered how I was going to avoid talking to Dan.

WE ARRIVED at the police station a few minutes later. It was in an uproar. Highly organized, but crazed. Everyone was busy. In the center of the whirlwind stood Dan, with Tyler following him like a shadow. "Detective Lockheart, she's not answering any of her calls."

Dan nodded. "We're looking into it, officer, now please, give me some space."

As the doors dropped closed behind us, Dan looked up and met my eye. He jabbed a finger in my direction and then pointed to the conference room. Immediately my blood boiled.

"I think he wants us to go to the conference room." Aerie tried to help.

"I know exactly what he means," I snapped. "Sorry, I don't mean to yell. He just makes me so mad when he does that." I hated being told what to do. Dan needed to realize pointing at me was like flame to a gasoline can.

"Yeah, I know. You said." She hooked her arm into mine and dragged me over to the conference room. Once the door had swung shut, the noise abated, and it was silent in the room. "It sounds like they can't find Tayla."

"Tyler looks very upset. I suppose we're to blame. I'm to blame."

"We're both to blame. It's not the first time we talked about a case in public. It's just the first time someone heard us that was involved."

I glanced out the glass window of the door. Tyler was red

in the face, and he was more animated than I had ever seen him. Dan was trying to calm him down. He was doing an admirable job about it too. I would give him that. But I was still mad at him. I hated being told what to do. Most of all from Dan. And finger pointing at me? Just. No.

After about five minutes I grew edgy. "I think he's making us sit here for nothing."

"He's just busy. Relax. He'll get to us when he can."

"Why are you always so patient with him?"

"I don't know," she said with a grin. "He is a good guy. Deep down, he really cares. He's been that way ever since high school."

"Has he always been bossy, too?"

Aerie appeared to think it over. "No. I think the bossiness started about..." She tapped her chin. "...about the time you showed up in town."

"What is that supposed to mean?"

"What do you think it means? You can't be that slow."

"I have no idea what you're talking about." Because I didn't. That's what I told myself, anyway.

"He likes you, Mira."

"No, he doesn't." I shook my head.

"Of course, he does. Why do you think he was talking to your sister?"

"That was my sister poking her nose into business she shouldn't. I don't need someone watching over me every minute of my life."

"Pretty sure that's not what Dan has in mind. He sincerely likes you. You can't tell?"

"No. I don't know what you're talking about." I stood and paced.

"Dan behaving this way around you is proof that he really likes you."

I looked at Aerie like she was crazy.

"I'm serious. If you asked him out on a date he would go. In a heartbeat."

"No, he wouldn't. Besides I just told you, I don't need someone looking out for me all the time."

"What do you think I do?"

"You're my friend."

"Yes. Exactly. That's what friends do."

"You never tell me what to do."

"No. But I do watch out for you."

Aerie was a very good friend. Memories of her taking care of me the night I sprained my ankle came to mind. "Thank you. I'm still not dating Dan."

"Why not?" She whined.

"Because I have awful luck with men. I don't need more drama in my life than I already have."

"What if it's the good kind of drama?"

"Good kind? There's a good kind?"

"Yeah. I have that with Sam. And it would be nice if you could have it to."

"Said like a true friend who would like her friend to be in the same boat. No thanks, I don't need the drama."

"You're missing out. Just imagine Dan giving you a kiss."

At that exact moment detective Dan Lockhart entered the room.

A picture of him leaning in to kiss me popped into my mind. My throat constricted and I couldn't breathe. I felt my cheeks flush.

"Are you okay, Mira?" Dan asked.

I waved a hand in front of my face. "It's just a little hot in here."

Aerie stifled a giggle.

This was all her fault.

Dan pulled out the seat at the table across from us. He took a deep breath and put the folder he was holding down on the table. "Occasionally the two of you together have been very helpful in the past. For that I'm very grateful. But..."

Here is where I would normally jump all over Dan for saying *but* about our help, however, thanks to Aerie's crazy visual of him kissing me, I didn't trust myself to say a single word. I gulped.

"Informing Tyler that his sister might be pregnant, well, that's a new low."

Now I couldn't help it. "A new low? We didn't know he was sitting right behind us."

"Is that even a subject you should have been discussing in public?"

"No, we were at Sam's. It's like a second home..." My voice trailed off. There was no good way to spin this and I felt terrible.

"Look no matter what you say I am not happy that you shared that questionable information with Tyler. I was already keeping tabs on Tayla as a part of this investigation. Now he is an emotional mess that I have to manage as well. I don't appreciate it.

"You obviously didn't keep tabs on Tayla. From what it looks like, you can't find her either."

Dan took a deep breath. "No. We can't seem to locate her whereabouts. At the moment."

I was about to say something when Dan cut me off.

"No. I don't want the two of you doing any more investigating into this. Leave this to the department. Someone is dead and someone is missing. It's dangerous."

I pointed out the conference room window. "Tyler is a

train wreck out there. I highly doubt he's going to be able to help you. You need us."

"Not on this investigation." He stood. "I'll see you two out."

"You don't want to know what we found out?"

"No."

"You're stubborn." I stood up.

"We visited Kurt's house his car is there but he's not home," Aerie said.

"Thanks for that. I'll see you both at the diner." He opened the conference room door.

I was about to scream at him when Aerie hooked her arm into mine and dragged me out of the police station.

"How can you ever think that I would date him?" I asked, exasperatedly.

"The two of you push the other's buttons. What can I say? But I think it's best case if we stay away from Dan until we solve this case."

"No kidding." I was now hot and grumpy.

"Come on let's have some of your raspberry sorbet to cool off."

"That I can agree to." We headed to the diner.

12

I tossed and turned all night, feeling guilt about how the day had gone. The next morning, I woke to this sound of screeching brakes. Like those on a big truck. I peered out the window to find a delivery truck parked behind Babs. I jumped out of bed and ran to the bathroom to splash my face with cold water. The appliances were here. And worse... Jay had pulled up in his truck and parked on Main Street. I brushed my teeth furiously. I pulled my hair back in a quick ponytail and threw on some sweatpants, that, thank the heavens, I had recently washed.

I entered the dining room just as the knock sounded on the door.

"Who is it? Who is it?" If I weren't already awake, Taco's squawk reverberating around my brain would have done the trick.

"It's Jay," a voice on the other side of the door answered as I pulled it open.

"Sorry, Taco..." I shook my head in frustration.

"I like your bird." He grinned when he noticed the bright red macaw.

"Be careful what you say; that's how I ended up with him."

"It's a big day today. You finally get your kitchen. Are you excited?"

I was more stressed out about Jay seeing me half-awake with the screeching macaw in the background. But I smiled. "Very excited. Come in." I shook my head at my slow hospitality.

"I can have the guys bring the appliances in through your kitchen's back door. That might be easier."

"Sure, no problem, I'll go open it."

Jay disappeared outside and I walked through the newly painted kitchen with its bright, cheerful, soft yellow walls and dove gray cabinets. I'd soon be able to cook in here. It was finally happening. My home would finally feel like mine once I could create yummy things in the kitchen.

I unlocked the back door and held it open while Jay and Devon brought the refrigerator in first. They wheeled it in with the cardboard box still draped over the top. I figured, to protect it from getting scratched in transit. But when Jay pulled the box away, I realized something was wrong. "This isn't the refrigerator I ordered."

Jay just stood there grinning.

"This is the expensive one." The refrigerator that stood before me was the top-of-the-line—all the bells and whistles—a brand that I could, no way, in any lifetime, afford.

Jay cleared his throat. "Dan and I went in together and upgraded your appliances as a thank you."

"What? Why?"

"To thank you for all the work that you do for the town. You deserve it."

"You and Dan?" I couldn't fathom why Dan would want

to buy me anything, although the practicality of it did sound like him. Jay originally asked me to dream big about the new kitchen back when we were standing in the rubble after the fire.

"Yeah, the two of us wanted to do something nice for you. Do you like it?" Jay looked concerned.

"I love it. Thank you so much." I didn't know how I could possibly accept it, but it was already in my kitchen, and I knew Jay would not take 'no' for an answer.

Jay leaned over and gave me a hug. A hug!

My brain raced through eight million different things all in the same millisecond. I wish I had showered; *I wish I had fixed my hair. Gosh, his arms are strong. I can't breathe because of my nerves. Is this hug still going on, is this real? Or am I dreaming?* I closed my eyes.

Jay stepped back. "I'm glad you like it. Dan wasn't sure if you'd think it was too much."

"No. No. I love it. This kitchen is now awesome with this refrigerator."

"Well, we also upgraded the other things, too."

"What?" I shook my head. "You guys upgraded everything?"

"Well, yeah. Why not?" He shrugged it off, in high spirits.

"Because it's expensive."

"Aw." He punched me softly in the arm. "You're worth it. We'll bring in the oven next."

I stood there in shock, shaking my head. Dan and Jay upgraded my appliances. Sometimes I just didn't understand men.

After they brought in the oven, a commercial six burner, the microwave oven, and the high-end blender, which I hadn't purchased, they installed everything and verified that it worked, Devon handed me the manuals, short one-page items that had the website to download the actual manuals.

When it looked like they were wrapping up, I thanked them both. "Thank you, guys. I really appreciate this."

Jay turned to Devon. "You can head back to the site. I'll be there in a few minutes. I need to talk to Mira."

"No problem." He waved to me. "Enjoy your new kitchen." He turned to Jay. "See you back at the site." Devon left out the back door. I heard the oversized delivery truck start up and drive away.

I watched Jay for a moment. Wondering why he wanted to talk to me alone. He tested the burners each one in turn. And then turned them off and faced me. "Are you sure you like it? Dan wasn't so sure. But you told me what you imagined this kitchen to be."

"I remember." I grinned, that first week I had been in town and met Aerie and Jay had been eventful. "This is exactly what I imagined. You've got a great memory."

"Dan asked me if I thought it was a good idea. So, we both went all in. I really hope you don't mind."

"It's wonderful. I'm just surprised. I thought Dan hated my guts."

Jay looked shocked. "No. He doesn't *hate* you." The little inflection his voice made on the word hate, inferring a different word entirely to describe what Dan felt for me, frightened me a little. Like maybe Dan liked me? It was coming from Jay. Now my brain was scrambled. I couldn't think straight.

"Okay."

"Well, you have to sort that out with him."

"I was hoping that I'd be able to talk to you for a minute about something personal. If you don't mind."

Sure. What's going on?"

"It's about Chelsea." Jay stood taller and stepped away from the oven. "I wanted to get your opinion. I am having a hard time with her lately."

"Okay." This conversation was going from weird and awkward to even weirder and more awkward. If that was possible.

"She, well, I mentioned this to you before; she wants a baby."

"Okay."

"Well, I heard the rumor that everyone thinks Tayla is pregnant."

"News travels fast. Not surprised."

"Yeah well, I'm wondering if that's why she's telling me she wants to get pregnant like ASAP."

"I couldn't tell you if that's why."

"Yeah, I know. I guess what I'm wondering is that, well, I don't trust Chelsea now that I told her I want to wait until I'm married."

"I see."

"And I think I should break up with her."

All the air left my lungs. My lips moved without making a sound. "Do you think that's a good idea?" I finally said.

He was standing in my newly finished dream kitchen that I never thought I'd own. With all his hotness, telling me that another guy liked me, and asking me if he should break up with my best friend's nemesis. Was I in an alternate universe?

"Do I think that's a good idea?" I repeated the question, knowing full well I sounded like my awful macaw Taco. I just needed a moment to compose myself.

"I don't know. I'm serious about waiting until we're married to have a kid. She's pretty adamant she doesn't want to wait. And I don't trust her."

"Trust is really important in a relationship." I knew from past experience how important trust could really be.

"Yeah. You're right. Trust is really important."

"Maybe you should just talk to her about the trust first and see what she has to say." I knew that was a non-answer. But I couldn't honestly say I could give Jay unbiased advice on his love-life. Mainly because I couldn't shake my Jay-crush. And I wasn't sure if I wanted to.

AFTER MY CONVERSATION WITH JAY, I knew I had to do two things. One was to confront Dan and find out why he would pay to upgrade my appliances with Jay. I knew they were friends, but I didn't expect Jay to strong-arm Dan into doing something like that. Secondly, I had an idea that I needed to talk to Chelsea. She was friends with Tayla, enough to know that she was pregnant before anybody else; she might also know where Tayla had gone. As much as I hated the idea of talking to Chelsea, I was investigating this to help a friend, and I was determined to get to the bottom of things. Even if it meant groveling to Chelsea.

For a moment I thought about telling Aerie. Unfortunately, having her come with me might cause more problems than help. So, I decided to go alone. It was hard to tear myself away from my amazing kitchen. It would still be there when I got back, I promised. Unless another fire broke out, of course. I knocked on every single piece of wood I could find after that disturbing thought. I locked the house up tight.

When I arrived at Chelsea's house, it appeared that she was leaving. She had keys in her hand and was heading toward her car.

"What do you want?" Her tone let me know I was thoroughly imposing on her time. But that tone was the only one Chelsea ever really used with me.

"Can we talk?"

"No. I'm on my way out. The girls and I are having brunch. Not at your diner."

"I wouldn't think so. Look, I really need to talk to you about Tayla."

"I shouldn't have said anything to you two and I regret it already. I can't talk to you about her at all."

I scanned the neighborhood and noticed a nosy older neighbor slowly getting her newspaper. I knew an eavesdropper when I saw one. "Can we go inside for a moment?"

Chelsea kept walking toward her car.

"I'll put in a good word for you with Jay."

She stopped in her tracks. I watched as she gripped her keys tighter making her knuckles white. "Fine. But make it fast." She turned around and opened her front door and we walked inside.

Her home was another average sized Victorian, standard in Pleasant Pond. Probably one of the original homes. It had a slightly old-fashioned feel to it but the living room looked newly decorated.

Chelsea threw her keys on the kitchen table. "Start talking. I don't have all day. There's fashionably late and then there's everyone's peeved at me. Brunch is waiting."

I didn't bother sitting down at the dining room table but stood and rested my hands on the back of a chair. "Look, I know you are good friends with Tayla. She might be in some trouble. I really need to talk to her if you know where she is."

"Dan-the-detective, already stopped by here and asked

me for directions on where he could find her. I said nothing to him. Why do you think I would say anything to you?"

"Because she could be framed for murder. I don't think she did it; probably not, anyway."

"She didn't kill Vicki. If that's what you're saying."

"Well, I agree. It's not looking that way by the evidence. So, if you know where she is I'd like to talk to her and try to figure out what's going on. That information could lead us to who the murderer really is."

"I promised her I wouldn't tell anybody where she is and I'm not going to tell you."

"I want to help her, Chelsea."

"So, you say."

"I won't tell Dan, if that's what you're worried about. I just need to ask her a few questions. You can come with me."

Chelsea looked me up and down. "She's my best friend." She paused for a moment. I hoped she was changing her mind.

"Then let me help her."

"You better not be lying." She squinted her eyes, scrutinizing me.

"You can come with me."

"Fine, I'll drive." She snatched her keys off the table and stormed out the front door. I followed her, pulling her front door shut and making sure it was locked. Hoping this was the lead that we needed, I hopped in the passenger side of Chelsea's car. I was surprised that helping a friend ranked above going to a social brunch. Maybe Aerie and I had been too hard on her.

After driving for twenty minutes, I had a flash of a thought that maybe Chelsea was pranking me. A good joke on Mira. I glanced at her to see if she had that look like a cat playing with a toy. But she just stared at the road with a determined look on her face. Well, if she was messing with me, it only cost me time. And confirmation that she was as awful as we originally thought.

Chelsea slammed the brakes and made a hard left down a dirt road. Her car bucked as we inadvertently hit pothole after pothole. "Crap, my poor car."

"I know a guy over at the garage. He can take a look at it." She gave me a grimace but slowed the car's speed and kept driving.

"Are we almost there?"

"Yes," she snapped at me. "If you tell anyone, and she hates me for it, I will make your life a living..."

"I get it. I get it. I don't doubt you either."

We pulled up to a small, worn hunting cabin. I noticed a small shed in the back. "Is that what I think it is?"

"An outhouse? Yes. There is no plumbing." She looked disgusted.

Tayla's car was parked at the side of the cabin.

Something seemed off. I could tell Chelsea felt it too. That's when we noticed that Tayla's driver side door was hanging open. We got out of the car quickly and hurried over. I glanced inside the car just before Chelsea closed her door. It was empty. Nothing seemed out of the ordinary except for the fact that the door was left open. But a vibe hung in the air; it just didn't feel right. Chelsea was already making her way up the porch steps. I followed close behind.

13

———

Finding the door unlocked, we cautiously entered the cabin. It was dimly lit. The only light came from an open back door. After a quick glance around, I realized it had two rooms with a set of stairs along the wall that led to a loft.

The sparse furnishings included a long coffee table and an ancient, overstuffed couch. The cabin smelled of dust and disuse. And something else. That's when I heard a sound coming from the shadows in the far corner. My eyes adjusted and I saw Tayla huddled against the wall.

Chelsea ran to her. She glanced right and stopped short. "Oh my..." She turned toward me, with a look of panic and ran past me out the front door.

Tayla sat with her legs pulled up to her chest, crying. Her entire body shook.

"Tayla, are you okay?" I slowly approached her.

She shook her head back and forth, back and forth. She raised one finger and pointed off to my right. I noticed what I thought was a lumpy blanket on the floor. A non-moving, non-breathing lumpy blanket. "Kurt."

I guessed I would be talking to Dan sooner than I thought.

I pulled out my cell phone and called him.

The local authorities showed up first. I explained to them that Chelsea and I were friends of Tayla's and that we were checking up on her when we came upon the body. While they worked, I stepped out onto the porch where Chelsea sat on the porch swing.

"Are you okay?" Chelsea looked a little green around the gills.

While the EMTs helped Tayla to the ambulance, Chelsea got up, her legs a bit shaky. "She won't tell them; I should let them know about her pregnancy."

Tayla was still in shock and hadn't said a word to anyone.

Chelsea spoke briefly to the medical workers and then came back and took her seat on the swing next to me. "You're a good friend, Chelsea."

"I can't believe that's Kurt in there. Dead."

I nodded. There wasn't much to be said.

"How can you do it?" she asked.

"What do you mean?"

"Look for people who do these things?"

"I want to know why, and I want to make sure they go to jail."

Chelsea shook her head and shivered. "I couldn't do it. Not after what I saw in there, he was stabbed to death. You're a stronger person than me."

"You did okay, too. Taking care of Tayla."

"She'll be okay, right?"

"She will need her friends. But she should be okay." I noticed Dan finishing up a conversation with the authorities. I got up from the swing and walked over to him.

"Is Chelsea, okay?" he pointed in the direction of the cabin.

"She's a little shaken up but she'll be okay. How is Tayla?" I asked.

"The EMTs say she didn't suffer any injuries. She's just in shock."

"Are you allowed to investigate this?" I noticed police officers I didn't know moving around the scene.

"No. But I need to share information with them if I learn anything."

"That sounds like what I do."

Dan let a short-lived grin cross his face. "I can take you back if you need a ride home."

"I can ride home with Chelsea. I think she might need somebody to talk to."

Dan pinched his lips and nodded. "Can we talk for a minute, privately, Mira?"

We walked further distance away from the crowd of police.

"I know you're investigating. I didn't tell our friends over there that you're involved. But it's okay with me if you continue to do it." His grin made my stomach flutter, but his change in attitude gave me whiplash.

"Are you actually agreeing to let me help?" I couldn't believe what I was hearing.

"Yes. I'll share information with you if you will do the same. I want to get to the bottom of this as much as you do. But—and this is a big but—always do your detecting with a partner. This is the second body in this investigation. Deal?" His eyes were a light brown with green in them, and very sincere.

I took a breath. "Deal."

"Will you make sure Chelsea gets home safe?"

I nodded. "Sure."

"See you back in Pleasant Pond." He turned to walk away. But I had to say something.

"Hey Dan?"

"Yeah."

"Thanks. Thanks for everything. Everything." I was thanking him for a lot of things, but mostly I was thanking him for trusting in me. I made my way back up the steps of the porch. "Chelsea, are you ready to go? I can drive if you want."

She nodded and absently pulled her keys out of her purse and handed them to me.

"Okay, let's go."

Once we were in the car she asked, "Can we follow the ambulance over to the hospital? I'd like to be there for Tayla."

"I think that's a great idea." Besides being a support for Tayla, I might be able to ask some questions to get to the bottom of why she was at this rural cabin in the first place. And why Kurt was there too. And how he ended up dead.

By the time we got to the hospital, Tayla was already signing the discharge papers. When she saw Chelsea, she collapsed into her arms sobbing. "We were going to have a life together."

"Come on, we'll go to my place." Chelsea rubbed her friend's back. She glanced up at me. "You too. Your car is still at my house."

While we walked to the parking lot, I organized the many questions I had on my mind to ask Tayla. Her shock seemed real. It didn't appear that she could be the murderer, but then who was? Once we were in the car, I tentatively asked her, "Tayla why were you at the cabin?"

She sniffled. "It's where Kurt and I meet."

"Did you have a disagreement with him?"

"Yes. No. I mean, we had an argument over text, and we were going to talk it through."

"About being pregnant?"

"Yes, we were really stressed out about it."

"Did you drive to the cabin together?" I was trying to slowly ask her if she had witnessed the murder.

"No, I drove myself. He was meeting me. But when I opened the door..." She choked back a sob.

"Were there any other cars? Kurt's?"

"No. At first, I thought I was early. That he had got delayed for some reason. But then I found him..." Chelsea turned to her friend and rubbed her shoulder. "It's going to be okay."

"No. It's not. Kurt is dead." The tears overflowed down her cheeks. "What do I do now?"

"You can move in with me. I will take care of everything." Chelsea looked resolute as she continued to drive us back to town.

"Can you think of anyone that would want Kurt dead?" I asked.

"His soon-to-be ex-wife. Except that she's already dead," Chelsea added.

I looked at Tayla. "Can I ask you how long the two of you were having an affair?"

"It started last summer. Kurt swore he was going to leave Vicki. But when I told him I was pregnant, he freaked out."

"Freaked out how?"

"I don't know. He kept saying how it would be harder to

divorce Vicki now that there was proof he was having an affair."

I wanted to know what had been going on with Kurt and I thought about how siblings were sometimes the closest of friends. Someone you share your deepest secrets with. "Tayla, do you know if Kurt has any siblings?"

"He has two brothers. They don't live around here." I could see her discomfort and wondered what and how much had she shared with her own brother.

I made a mental note to interview Kurt's brothers when they arrived in town. Although I didn't know if I would get much information from them, it was still worth checking out.

Once we were back at Chelsea's house, I thanked her for the ride, and watched as she carefully took Tayla inside. I wrestled my keys out of my front pocket and hopped into Babs. I wanted to drive over to Aerie's and fill her in on everything that had happened. More importantly, I needed her input. I had no idea where to go from here. We were out of suspects.

14

────────

Aerie opened her door at the first knock. "Kurt is dead," I told her.

"Can we go over to your kitchen? I want to see the new appliances. Jay told me he and Dan upgraded them for you." She elbowed me in the side.

"I just told you that Kurt was killed. And that's your response?"

"Yeah, I know. Dan told Jay and Jay told me. You and I will need to go over and tell Heather. But first I want to see your new kitchen."

I shrugged. Aerie never ceased to surprise me. "Okay, let's go." After the requisite oohs and ahhs over my kitchen, we finally settled down in the dining room and I gave her the details.

"Chelsea was really the mother hen?" Aerie still couldn't believe me.

"She obviously has another side to her personality that we just haven't seen."

"Well, I'm glad somebody will be taking care of Tayla, she'll need the support."

"She does have a brother, you know. Or did you forget about Tyler?"

"I didn't forget about him. I just know that sometimes brothers can be a little judgmental. I'm glad that Tayla has a friend in Chelsea at least. Kind of like how I have you as my friend."

"Jay isn't judgmental, is he?"

"He is very overprotective, if you haven't noticed."

I remembered just how overprotective he was when Aerie started to date Sam. "I get your point." Plus, I had an overprotective sibling as well. That package. I pushed it to the back of my mind. We were in the middle of a murder investigation. Mail could wait.

"I just don't know where we are in this case. There are no more suspects."

"Obviously there's a suspect out there. We just need to figure out who it is." All of a sudden there was a squawk and Taco flew across the room. Arnold had let him out. I had wondered why Arnold had been hanging around the cage.

"He's a player, he's a player!" Taco squawked at full volume.

Arnold hissed and swatted at him, claws extended. I pointed to Arnold. "No. Bad kitty."

Then the fan in the kitchen fell with a thud and the window slammed shut with a bang.

I hate when you call me kitty. I also am not bad. That bird needs to go. He's much too loud; it ruins my nerves.

I glared at him and went to help Aerie who was trying to corral Taco.

Again, there was only one way to get Taco's attention. I walked back to his cage and sighed at my imminent humiliation. "I'll give you a kiss, Taco."

The huge scarlet macaw flew across the room and

landed on my outstretched arm. I leaned over and gave him a peck on the beak. He climbed back onto his perch. I closed the door and latched it. I frowned at Arnold. He was really trying my patience by opening Taco's cage.

"You now have a temporary ban on treats, Arnold." I shook my finger at him.

Aerie was in the kitchen returning the fan to the window.

Arnold rubbed his face against my shin. *The ghost made me do it.*

"A likely story."

"Why don't we go to Heather's and let her know about the new information."

I shrugged. "It can't hurt."

"We'll figure it out. We always do."

"But what if we don't this time?"

"What's with all the negative vibes?"

"I don't know, I just can't think of any other possible suspects. Dan even gave me carte blanche to work on this. And now I feel like I'm frozen."

"He what?"

"Yeah, I forgot to mention he can't work on Kurt's case because it's not in his jurisdiction, but he wants it solved just as badly as we do. He said he would share information as long as I did the same."

"Well, there you go. Have a conversation with Dan and see what he knows." She noticed me hesitating.

"You don't want to go talk to him because you don't know how to thank him for upgrading your kitchen appliances."

"It's weird."

"No, it's not. Jay and Dan are thanking you. Jay is just being a cool guy and Dan is...well, Dan likes you. And you helped him solve a lot of his cases recently. So, he's thanking you."

"That still doesn't change that it's weird. And I don't know what to say to him."

"Thank you would be a start."

"I suppose."

"And he could have information. Information that can help us solve the case. So, you have to go talk to him." Aerie was now all smiles and upbeat. "I'll talk to Heather. You go see Dan."

I let out all the air in my lungs and in a big huff. "Fine. But, like, text me in twenty minutes. That way I have a way out."

"You want me to fake text you so you can tell Dan you have to leave?"

"Yes, please."

"That's so lame." She shook her head.

"Please?"

"As long as you go talk to him."

I stuffed my phone in my back pocket. "You'll tell me if you learn anything from Heather?"

"You know I will. And you'd better tell me every single word Dan says to you."

"Okay. Here I go." I headed for the door. But you'll still text me in twenty minutes, right?"

"You're hopeless."

Once we were outside, I pulled the front door closed. I was off to talk to Dan.

WHEN I WALKED into the police station Dan noticed me right away and waved me back into the conference room. With the door closed, he looked at me expectantly." Have you learned anything new?"

"Not really. Just the obvious. Tayla and Kurt were having an affair. She's pregnant. He was upset about it and swore he was going to divorce Vicki."

"It's still a possibility that Kurt was the one who killed Vicki, and someone found out and killed him. We could be looking at two suspects."

"I don't think it was two people."

"What evidence do you have suggesting it's not?" he asked.

"Do you have evidence that says it is?"

"I'm still waiting for the analysis to come back from the lab regarding Vicki."

"Did you get any information from the authorities who took on Kurt's case?"

"Unfortunately, no. Nothing more than what we saw when we were there. Thank you again for calling me."

"You're the first person I thought of to call. I figured it was outside your jurisdiction, but I knew it would be helpful if you were there. Mostly because I feel that both of these murders are tied together."

"I'll continue to look into Vicki's murder. I have an interview with her father today. Would you like to come?"

Being invited to join Detective Lockhart on his investigation was a huge shift in our investigating relationship. "You trust me enough to join you with your investigation?"

I watched Dan hesitate ever so slightly before he replied, "Yes."

"You don't have to lie. You're buttering me up so I share more information with you. I get it.

"That's not true."

"That's okay, Dan, I understand. But you don't have to worry, I'll share whatever information I get. For Tayla's sake and for Heather's I want to see this investigation closed as much as you do."

Dan cleared his throat. "Well, I have to leave to meet with Vicki's father. You're welcome to come."

I wanted to know what Dan learned from Vicki's father. But I could find out later. I shook my head and walked out of the police station.

I couldn't believe I was turning down an invitation to sit in on Dan interviewing Vicki's father. And a voice in the back of my head reprimanded me for already breaking Dan's one rule of not going it alone. But I had a hunch. One that meant that I needed to talk to Kurt's brothers. A hunch that couldn't wait.

15

___

It didn't take much sleuthing to find Kurt's brothers at Kurt's and Vicki's home. Dan had obviously notified the family of his death. They had arrived to handle the property and funeral matters.

I knocked on the door and was surprised at how quickly it was answered.

"I'm assisting with the investigation into Vicki's and Kurt's murders. I'm wondering if you can help me with some information?" I asked.

"I'm Chad, Kurt's brother. This is Mark. Come on in."

"I'm hoping you have additional information you might be able to share," I said as I stepped into the home.

"Sure. Whatever we can do," Chad said.

"Did either of you know about Kurt's affair?"

Chad nodded. "I did."

Mark stared at him.

"What? He told me everything," Chad continued. "He got back in touch with the girl he dated in high school. The one he dated while on a break from Vicki."

"When did he tell you he was cheating on his wife?" Mark appeared to be truly upset at this news.

"This is why he didn't tell you," Chad said matter-of-factly.

Mark crossed his arms angrily. "He shouldn't be cheating on his wife. That's what got him in this situation."

Death was certainly a situation. "Can you tell me what he told you about the relationship?" My hunch was something related to the infidelity in this marriage had caused the murder. I just didn't see how, yet.

"I know the girl's name was Tayla. He told me he wasn't sure about leaving Vicki. I know he was having a hard time making that decision."

"So, you're saying he hadn't planned to divorce Vicki?"

"No. He hadn't gotten that far. He was trying to sort out his feelings, at least that's what our phone calls were about."

If Kurt wasn't planning on leaving Vicki, had he been planning on killing her instead? But in that scenario, who killed Kurt? I looked at Kurt's older brother, Mark. He seemed to feel that his brother got his just desserts for cheating on his wife.

"Had he mentioned details about Tayla to either of you?"

"No. He was pretty stressed out about whether or not to tell Vicki. But again, I don't think he was planning on divorcing Vicki for her."

"I just can't believe this happened. That they're both dead." Mark shook his head.

"I'm sorry this has happened to your family. We're doing our best to find the killer."

"Who would want them both dead?"

"That's what we intend to find out," I said.

"Thank you." Mark shook my hand. Chad took a deep

breath. "I can't believe he's gone." He pinched the bridge of his nose and turned away.

"I'll be in touch if we find out anything."

"Thank you, again." Mark closed the door silently between us.

I took a deep breath. Other than learning about brotherly dynamics in Kurt's family I hadn't learned much that would help in the search for the murderer. Except that Kurt didn't have any plans to leave Vicki. Making Tayla look a bit more suspicious.

I think it was time to sit down with Aerie and brainstorm. We needed to review all the clues that we had.

I TEXTED Aerie before I drove home. *You didn't rescue text me!*

Sorry. Not sorry. Did you survive?

Yes. And I have info from Kurt's brothers.

She agreed to meet at my house.

Aerie stood on my front stoop with Heather. "We need another set of eyes on this to figure it out."

"Sounds good." I sighed as I opened the door. Arnold and Ozzie came running. After all that happened this morning, I could definitely use some puppy love and kitty snuggles.

"You look really tired." Aerie peered at me.

"I know you mean that in a maternal kind of way. But yeah, this morning was pretty rough."

Heather petted Arnold and then sat at the dining room table. "When you went into the cabin, he was dead? Did Tayla do it?"

"My first impression was that she didn't. But she does have a motive." After giving the animals treats, I sat at the table. "I just got back from interviewing Kurt's brothers. One of them didn't know about the affair and the other was under the impression that Kurt did not plan on leaving Vicki for Tayla."

"Did either of them know about Tayla being pregnant?"

"No."

"You think he was hiding it from his brother?"

"He was either hiding it or he hadn't had time to tell him. While one of his brothers was upset with him and the other one was supportive, I don't think either of them would've killed Kurt."

Aerie pulled out a notebook and a pen. "Let's make a new list of all the suspects. I think we need to start from the beginning."

"Yes, because other than a hunch that the two murders were done by the same person, the only suspect I can think of is Tayla."

"It makes perfect sense if she knew that Kurt wasn't leaving his wife, then she would want to get rid of Vicki. All the more motive to kill her."

I shook my head. "But you didn't see her at Kurt's murder scene. She was really upset."

"Maybe they got in a fight, and she defended herself?"

"Something just doesn't sit right about the whole thing. I can't put my finger on it."

"Let's start from the beginning. We know that Tayla and Vicki had a fight at GNO the night before Vicki was found dead at your pottery place, Heather." Aerie wrote this down in the notebook.

"We know the Vicki's father is a lawyer who represents bad guys. So, there's a possibility of a suspect there."

"Dan is meeting with Vicki's father now to interview him. He said he'll let me know what he finds out."

"Wow, that's new. How did you get him to do that?"

"Don't insinuate something happened between us. I told him I would share any information I get, and he said he would do the same. That's it. That's all. Nothing else happened."

"Okay." Aerie said it like she didn't believe me.

"Then somewhere around this time we learn Tayla is pregnant. And that maybe Kurt wasn't so excited about it."

"His brother did mention Kurt hadn't made up his mind about leaving Vicki."

"Another reason Tayla could be the murderer."

"I guess." The brainstorming wasn't helping. "I still feel like we are missing something."

My phone beeped. A text from Dan popped up: *I might've found something.*

"Dan says he might have something." The phone beeped again. "He's on his way over."

Aerie stood up. "We'll go."

Heather looked like she wanted to stay.

"We need to leave the lovebirds alone," she told Heather. "Don't worry, Mira will tell us everything," Aerie turned to me and shook her finger. "And I mean everything." She picked up her notebook. "Come on, Heather. We'll go over the notes at my house."

"Bye, guys. I'll let you know what he says."

"Or does." Aerie pulled the door shut.

Can I have more treats? Arnold purred as he rubbed against my leg.

"I give you treats if you promise to stop letting the bird out of the cage."

I told you, Clara makes me do it.

"I have a hard time believing anyone makes you do anything, Arnold."

You're right. She doesn't make me do it; she suggests I do it, and I wholeheartedly agree. Because it's fun watching that bird fly. Because one day that bird will fly out the window and I won't have to hear his extremely loud and annoying squawking anymore.

I put a little pile of treats on the floor to appease Arnold. Then I spotted the box Darla had sent me on the floor next to the table leg. I must have put it there at some point when I was cleaning off the table.

I PICKED up the box and sat at the dining room table. It was about time I opened the thing. I had this sensation right now that I absolutely needed to do it. I wondered if this was how Darla's psychic skills worked. That hunch I had earlier, that super-strong hunch to do something. Or maybe I was just plain curious. What had Darla sent me out of the blue? I left the box sitting on the table and retrieved a butter knife from the kitchen. I barely gave my brand-new kitchen a thought. That's how much I suddenly wanted to open this box. I slid the blade around the edges of packing tape and finally cut down the center, peeling open the flaps. Whatever it was, she had wrapped it in colorful tissue paper. In between the folds of paper, I found a dark blue velvet bag. I lifted it from the box. The bag was heavier than it looked.

I pulled open the drawstring and poured the contents into my hand. A number of polished stones tumbled out.

"What am I supposed to do with these?" A piece of paper was stuck to the bottom of the bag. "Don't Trust the Player?" I flipped the paper over and back again. That was it? "Could you get any more cryptic?" I shouted to the ceiling.

Just then the fan fell away from the kitchen window and the window slammed shut. Frustration lit every nerve in my body. "Clara, if that is you, please stop doing this to the fan. I hear you!"

I sat down hard in the chair. What was I doing? Following hunches? Talking to ghosts? Goodness, I was turning into my sister!

I took a deep breath. The stones lay scattered on the table where I had let them fall when the fan crashed to the floor. What was I supposed to do with a bunch of stones? I wasn't the psychic in the family. What good would stones do me? Already the room was warming up from the kitchen window being closed. I pushed away from the table and went into the kitchen. I lifted the window and shoved the fan back in.

The breeze from outside was more than welcome. I stood there breathing in for a moment. Same thing happened when Jay was here painting. And when I first got the package from Darla. If it really was Clara pushing the fan out over and over again, what was her reasoning? Why at those moments? I took another deep breath, headed back to the dining room and sat. I gathered up the stones and put them back in the velvet pouch then stuffed it into the cardboard box that it was delivered in. Crystal stones are not going to help me with this murder mystery. Not this time; not any time.

Sensible logic could save the day. I was sure of it. I was just stuck.

A knock pounded on the door. I nearly jumped out of my skin. I almost forgot that Dan was coming over. I suddenly felt nervous. The last time he had been at the house I had kicked him out. Hopefully this visit would go better.

I opened the door to find him typing into his phone.

He glanced up.

"Come in." I offered him a seat at the dining room table. "What did you learn from interviewing Vicki's father?"

"Not much. He hasn't been practicing law for a number of years and he has no idea of anyone prior to that that would want to harm his family."

"Another dead-end. I spoke with Kurt's brothers. Only one of them knew about the affair with Tayla. The other was very judgmental."

I didn't know why Dan would say that he might have found something and the answer was nothing. All of Aerie's teasing about Dan liking me came to mind. "Neither knew about the pregnancy."

"Maybe either or both could be suspects?"

"I didn't get that impression. Both of them were equally upset." I saw by the look on Dan's face that he was out of leads too. "I know we are missing something. I just don't know what."

We sat there staring uncomfortably.

"Do you want something to drink?" I had forgotten all my good hosting skills.

"That would be great. Thank you. Ice water is fine. Mind if I help?"

I shrugged nervously. He followed me into the kitchen. And then I realized. He wanted to see the appliances. I totally forgot to thank him. "Dan, Jay told me about how you guys upgraded my appliances. I really appreciate it. It was lame of me not to mention it earlier."

Dan smiled humbly. "It's nothing. Just a thank you." He

looked up at the refrigerator. "Looks good. I'm glad you have your kitchen back."

"I haven't been able to use it yet." I fake laughed.

"Between working at the diner and helping with the investigation I can imagine you've been a little bit busy."

Awkward silence again. Then I remembered the water. I pulled two glasses and filled them at the tap. "Let's see if the icemaker works."

Dan stood near the refrigerator. I tried to relax even though he stood so close to me I could touch him. I pushed my glass under the icemaker in the refrigerator door. A churning sound and two ice cubes plopped into my glass of water, splashing Dan across his midsection.

"Oh my gosh, I'm so sorry."

Dan chuckled. "It's fine." He brushed at the water. "It's just water. And, hey, the icemaker works."

I handed him his glass. He took a sip. More awkward silence.

My mind drifted to the murder, specifically Vicki's murder. If we are missing something... "We should start at the beginning," I blurted out.

"What?" Dan was startled from his thoughts. Had he been focused on me instead of the refrigerator?

I cleared my throat. "We should start at the beginning of the investigation. We should go back to Heather's shop and review all the evidence that we already have. If we are missing something, it's going to be there."

"You're right, Mira. We should start at the beginning. After a glass of water." He lifted his glass and I lifted mine to his and with a clink the plan was set.

16

It was decided Dan would go back to the precinct and look over all of the evidence the police had collected. I would go back to Heather's shop and interview her again about Vicki, and that night specifically.

Heather waved as she saw me exit my car and head for her door. "Hey, Mira. I didn't expect to see you back here."

"Dan and I had a quick talk. He wasn't able to find out any more information. So, we're kind of stuck."

Heather shook her head. "How can I help?"

"Can we talk about the party again, anything out of the ordinary in general. Anything about Vicki. I'm just trying to find something we've missed. Something we're all overlooking."

Heather nodded. "I understand."

We sat at one of the small square tables in the middle of the pottery shop. I glanced around the room. She had done a good job of restocking the shelves after the incident. "The place is looking better."

"Thanks. I have another delivery coming today. And

then we'll have the inventory back to where it was before… you know…Kurt's visit."

"That's great to hear." I took out my notebook and opened it to a fresh page, determined to find this elusive piece of information that was hiding from us. "Let's start with Vicki. When did you first meet her?"

I wrote everything down. Every word. Until my hand cramped. I stopped to stretch my fingers and shake out my arm when the shop door opened. "More packages for you, Heather." The delivery guy walked in pushing a dolly with two large boxes.

"Great. Thanks, Brad. They can go into the back room. I'll unbox them later."

"Sure thing." I watched as Brad pushed the boxes and disappeared down the hallway to the storage room. He returned moments later and asked Heather to sign for the delivery. Heather quickly scribbled her name.

"Thanks, Brad." She smiled at him.

"No problem. You have a nice day."

As the deliveryman left the shop, he winked at me. That guy was such a player. And just as soon as I thought it, my breath stopped. A player. *Don't trust the player.*

I had to ask Heather, "Do you get packages often? I mean before Kurt wrecked everything?"

"Probably twice a month."

"Is it always the same person?" I could feel I was on to something.

"Brad? Yeah," she said.

"Is it always Brad?" I pressed.

"Yes. I think so." A look of concern crossed her face.

"When did Vicki come to the shop?" An idea formed.

"Once a week. Like clockwork, she was here each week."

"Do you remember which day of the week?"

"Thursdays."

"Is it the same day you got deliveries?"

"To be honest I don't really pay attention when I get the deliveries, only that I get them. You know, to keep track of inventory."

"Can we check on your computer when the packages arrived?"

Heather nodded and we walked over to her computer at the front of the room. "Ha. That's odd."

"What is?"

"All my deliveries happened on a Thursday. Regardless of when I placed the order."

"How well do you know Brad?" I asked.

"I don't." Heather was coming to the same conclusion.

"But you trust him to go into your back room?"

"Yeah. He's been the delivery guy for at least a year." Her voice grew quieter now.

"And Vicki has been coming here every Thursday for months?"

"Yes." The realization hit Heather at the same time.

"Can you promise not to say anything to anybody?"

She nodded.

"And don't place any orders."

"I won't," she said firmly.

"I'm going to talk to Dan."

She nodded again. As I left I could've sworn she locked the door behind me. I wasn't really going to talk to Dan though. I needed to find more evidence before I handed him this lead.

I COULDN'T WAIT to place an order and then wait for Brad to show up. I went straight to Aerie's. "Are you waiting on a delivery?"

"What are you talking about?" She noticed the look on my face. "I got a delivery of pasta and sauce this morning. Jay's on his way over—I've finally convinced him to have a brother-sister heart-to-heart about what's going on in his life."

"Was Brad the one who made the delivery?"

"What is this all about?" She looked equally concerned and curious.

"I'm trying to figure out his route. I need to confront him."

"You think he's the one that killed Vicki? And Kurt? And you want to confront him?" She shook her head like I was crazy.

"It's a lead. I need to get some evidence."

"What kind of evidence?"

"The good kind," I said.

"Ha, ha, that usually means trouble."

"Usually. I need to get into the back of the guy's truck. There could be evidence in there. And if there is then we've caught our killer." I already felt triumphant.

Aerie put her hand on her hip. "Are you trying to impress Dan?"

I thought for a moment. "Yes."

"Give me a minute. I'll text and cancel with Jay."

"Don't cancel. You've been waiting to talk with him. This is probably nothing. I'll text you if something gets weird."

"Don't get yourself killed," she said in a motherly tone.

"Words of wisdom from my bestie."

"You better listen to me. Don't get killed!" she shouted as I left.

"I've got my phone. I'll text you if I find anything," I shouted over my shoulder. First, I needed to figure out where this Brad guy was.

17

A delivery van was parked outside the bank. Our delivery guy, Brad, was walking out of the building.

I hopped in Babs my Buick, determined to follow this guy. I waited until he was a few hundred yards down the road before I pulled up behind him. Finding him so quickly could only be ascribed to pure luck. But now I had to figure out how I could get into the back of his truck to look for evidence.

We were about five or six miles outside of town on one of the winding two lane roads, when the delivery van pulled over and stopped. For a moment I thought I would just have to drive past and find another way to get the evidence I needed. I was so close. And he was right here. I pulled up behind the van and put Babs in park.

Brad hopped out of the truck and walked purposefully toward my car.

I wanted to rehearse what I would say to him, but nothing came to mind. Not a single thing or reason that I could come up with as to why I was following him. Maybe I could tell him that I was impatient for a package? Hey, I've done dumber things.

I rolled down my window.

"Are you following me?" He smiled a bright shining smile and flexed his biceps as he put his hands on his hips. "I get off my shift in another hour." He winked. He was definitely a player, and he was definitely hitting on me.

"I'm waiting on a package. It's kind of urgent." I showed him my best smile. I sucked at flirting so I wouldn't bother trying.

"Well, let's take a look in the back. We'll see if we can find your *package* for you." He winked again. This was my chance to look for evidence. I wondered if I could take out my phone and hide it and take photos once he opened the doors. It would be too obvious if I did that right now. Maybe as we got closer...

Brad walked in front of me and unlatched the doors to the back of the truck. He hopped inside. "Your name is Mira, right? You live on Market Street."

"Yeah, that's right." It was a little more than creepy that he knew where I lived. But he was a delivery truck driver. He probably knew where everyone lived.

I tried to peer inside the van but the contrast between the bright summer sun and the dark interior made it difficult.

"Come on up. You can help me look."

Perfect. I could hop inside, take out my phone and take some quick photos. I climbed into the van and pretended to look at the boxes. With my back to him, I slowly pulled out my phone. A sudden intense pain hit me across the side of my head. I stumbled into a sharp edge of a box. Everything went dark. I could have sworn I heard the peep of chicks.

When I opened my eyes, my hands were bound with

packing tape, the van doors were closed, and we were speeding down the rural two-lane road.

I was lying flat on my back on top of my hands. The truck jostled and bounced me into hard packages. Yep, I could still hear the chirp and peeps of chicks. Somewhere in one of these boxes were some fluffy little baby chickens. I pushed my sneakered feet against the floor so I could sit up and take the weight off my hands. A box next to me fell and broke open. Two dozen fuzzy little chicks chirped and pecked around my legs. Oh, boy.

What had I been thinking? He hadn't been hitting on me. He knew I was looking into the murder. And now I was trapped in the back of his truck. Dan was right to tell me not to investigate alone. Aerie told me not to get killed. Even Taco told me not to trust the player. And still I had run straight into danger. But I discovered the killer. I just needed to find my way out before I was next.

DWELLING on how dumb I had been to get inside of Brad's truck with my back turned to him wouldn't get me out of this situation. Kurt's brother had called death "a situation". I anxiously giggled.

Focus, I told myself.

I had to find a way to get out. But it also wouldn't hurt if I happened to stumble across some evidence while I was in here. I worked hard to get in this stupid truck. I was determined to find the evidence we needed. And, of course, make it out alive. That was also important.

I pressed my back against the wall of boxes and tried pulling my hands apart. But they were securely taped up to my elbows with plastic packing tape. And it was quickly cutting off my circulation. The packing tape across my lips was firmly in place. But at least I could breathe through my nose.

I remembered now that the first victim, Vicki, had been found with packing tape around her wrists. A shiver ran down my spine. I would not end up like Vicki.

Where was my phone? I could tell it was no longer in my back pocket. I glanced around the truck bed. I squirmed attempting to look between the boxes. The chicks were all over the place. "Be careful you guys." I didn't see my phone anywhere. Great. Brad had my phone.

On top of one of the boxes was a packing tape gun. The blue handle stuck out over the edge of the box in front of me, a little higher than eye level.

That could definitely be evidence. And the tape gun had its own serrated edge to cut tape. I needed to get close enough to it to cut the tape off of my wrists. I squirmed around again on the floor—avoiding the fuzzy critters—to get my feet under me, thankful again for all the times Aerie pushed me to go to yoga class. Because some of these contortions were definitely yoga-worthy. Again, I pressed my back against the boxes, pushed my feet against the floor, and tried to stand. The tape at my knees didn't help matters. I teetered precariously as I made my way closer to the carton with the tape gun.

Suddenly the truck screeched to a stop. My body slammed hard into the pile of boxes next to me, crushing most of them. The little peeps slid forward and tumbled but managed to huddle together. I hoped nobody was expecting an order of fine china today. I slid down the boxes with my back on the floor. My hands throbbed and I struggled to push myself up.

"Stay put little fish, I'll be back. I have a job to do, you know. I can't stop to play." Brad actually smiled and grabbed a package. I watched as he exited out the front passenger side of the truck.

I screamed through taped lips. He actually had the nerve to continue with his deliveries. He was more arrogant than I thought. I kept screaming. But no one could hear me. The engine on the truck continued to run and I knew the sound was covering up my muffled, tape-covered shouts.

I took a deep breath in through my nose, thankful for Aerie's yoga classes where she taught us about controlling our breath. It helped me to calm myself down. I had to keep my wits about me if I was going to get out of this alive.

18

I got my feet under me again and balanced myself against the boxes I had crushed. I leaned forward and fell onto the box holding the packing tape, knocking the gun onto the floor. The only way I would be able to use the packing tape gun to cut the tape from my arms was if I somehow managed to lean back on top of the tape gun. I squirmed and inched and squirmed and inched some more until the roll of tape and the plastic handle dug into my lower back. I listened hard for any sound that Brad was returning. I thought I heard giggling. Was he really flirting with some woman while he had me in the back of the truck? He definitely was a player. And a murderer. I had to get out of here.

I pressed my arms against the tape roll until I felt the serrated edge dig into my skin. Then I felt the tape catch. I was getting out of this truck.

That's when Brad showed up. And he was way too cheery. "Hello, little fish. I have one more stop and then we can have some fun." He swiveled in his seat to focus on driving.

I furiously rubbed my arms against the serrated edge of the tape roll.

I tugged and pulled on the tape until I barely had feeling in my fingers. I was determined to get my arms free before his next stop.

The truck lurched to a halt way too soon. But tape was loose at my wrists. Brad leaned in to grab another box and I froze. I couldn't let him know what I was doing.

He stared at me for a long moment. "You're being so patient. We're almost done." He grabbed the carton and closed the door with a slam. I yanked at my wrists until the plastic finally gave way. I let out a sigh after I peeled the tape off my mouth. I twisted around and grabbed the tape gun and was using it to cut the tape from my knees when Brad hopped back into the driver seat.

I held onto the tape gun. It was my only weapon. That's when he saw me.

"Whoa now, what do you think you're doing?"

I unlatched the back doors and jumped out, practically falling on my face. I could barely feel my feet, but I was pretty sure I'd sprained my ankle. Again. I hobbled up to stand just as Brad came around to face me, holding an open box cutter. I held tight to the tape gun and swung it at his head but missed as he dodged.

"You were having an affair with Vicki, weren't you? That's why she was always at Pocket Moon Pottery."

"Yeah? Why? Do you want some of this action?"

"Don't make me sick." I swung at his head again. This time he wasn't expecting it and I clocked him solidly at the temple. He staggered. I took off running toward a house. My legs refused to cooperate, and I stumbled in the grass. Brad pushed me from behind and I fell forward. I vowed to go down swinging, I knew that for sure. But I was also determined to get a confession out of this guy. I rolled over in the grass to face him, and I struggled to get my feet under me. "Why did you kill Vicki? Did you get bored of her?"

"Of course, I got bored of her. She wanted to get married. She wanted to tell her husband about us and run away together."

Now I understood. "So that's why you had to kill Kurt. After you killed Vicki, you were afraid she told him about you, right?"

"That guy was too easy. I threatened to kill his girlfriend and he folded like a wimp." He shoved the box cutter close to my face. "Now let's get back into the van. We can't have any fun here." He glanced around the yard for spying eyes.

Having him tell me about his plan had been a good idea to stall for time but I still had no clue how to get out of this situation. I would have to use the last resort. I had to scream. My back was to the road when I heard a car pull up.

In seconds, Brad had me in a chokehold and stood me in front of him. I had never been so happy to see Dan's car in all my life. Although the cold sharp blade of the box cutter at my jugular kept me from grinning.

"LET HER GO." Dan walked toward us slowly with one hand on his holster. "I don't want to have to get my gun out. But I will if you don't let her go."

Scenarios of how this could play out danced through my mind.

Brad could continue to back up to the open truck doors and toss me inside. Would Dan be able to get to me before he drove off? Or would Brad get desperate? He already killed two people; he had nothing to lose. Here was Dan confronting him. The box cutter could slide across my throat in seconds. My legs, my hands, it felt like all of my extremities, were numb. Then I realized I still held the tape gun. Brad, in his eagerness to get me back in the truck had forgotten about it. I adjusted my grip, tightening my barely sensing fingers around the handle.

"Let her go, Brad. This doesn't have to get any worse." Dan's commanding voice didn't waver, but I saw the desperation in his eyes.

Brad dragged me closer to the truck. Dan positioned his hand at his hip for easy access to his gun.

I just needed Brad to back up one more step. I willed Dan not to pull out his weapon. I wanted Brad to still think he was getting out of this, to let his guard down.

I took a slow and even yoga breath. I gripped the barrel of the tape gun, bent my knees ever so slightly for balance, and heaved. I swung the tape gun in a wide arc while at the same time I pivoted my neck down and away from the box cutter. The tape gun made contact with Brad's face. That would leave a mark. I pushed off him and fell in the opposite direction.

Dan was already on top of him. Pinning him against the truck flipping him around and cuffing him. That's when I realized I was sitting in the gravel at the side of the road. I sucked in a ragged breath. I continued to sit there as Dan yanked Brad up and back to the patrol car, shoved him inside, and slammed the door.

Before I could even register that I might not be killed today, Dan had his hand out. "Are you okay? Let me help you up." I took his hand. He repeated, "Are you okay?"

My arms and legs were shaky. But I managed a smile. "I am now. Thanks." I let out a trembling breath. I felt like I was about to collapse. Dan seemed to notice. He slid his arm around my waist and took my right hand in his and walked me toward his car.

"Oh, wait," I stopped. "The chicks."

"The what?"

"Baby chicks in the back of the van." I managed to squeak out. Those poor little fuzzy birds.

"I'll take care of it." He opened his car door. I was grateful for the support of the passenger seat, and the view through the windshield of Dan attempting to corral two-dozen little fuzzy chicks. I couldn't decide who was cuter, the chicks or Dan being so very gentle with them.

19

One would think that sitting in the same patrol car as one's former captor would be a harrowing experience. Not for me. I felt a huge sense of accomplishment. I almost felt like gloating. Brad, the jerk, was behind me, cuffed and ready to go to jail.

"He confessed everything to me."

"I'm not surprised." Dan cleared his throat as if he was about to say more but he remained silent until we got to the police station. He asked me to sit in the conference room while he booked our perp.

Once that was complete, he came in quietly and sat across from me. "Mira," his voice was quiet. He closed his eyes. He took a slow, measured breath, and then looked at me. "I can't have you jeopardizing your safety like this anymore."

"But I got the bad guy."

Dan took another breath and chewed on his upper lip. "Look, Mira. I care about you. And seeing you with a knife to your throat almost made me lose my mind."

I couldn't argue, or tease him, or pick a fight. What could I say?

"Promise me. You'll stop investigating crimes."

I narrowed my eyes and looked at him. "I'm not going to stop. I find criminals. They end up in jail. Because I did the work." There was a desperate sound in my voice. Did I really need this investigating business to be happy? The answer was, yes. Finding the bad guy, putting them away—it made me feel good, like I was helping. I needed that.

The look of desperation was still in Dan's eyes. But I couldn't say anything to rid him of that. "I have to keep doing this."

"No. You don't have to keep doing this, and I forbid you to do this ever again."

I stood quickly. Knocking the chair over behind me. "You can't forbid me to do anything!"

"Mira." Dan's voice dropped to a quieter, urgent tone.

"No, Dan. You don't get to say what I can do. I'm going to continue to help the community when any crime happens. Because I just have to."

Dan pinched his lips together. He hung his head as I walked past him and out of the conference room. I didn't stop walking until I made it back to the house. My legs were shaking as bad as they were after the incident with Brad. As I got inside the house, I collapsed into a chair in my dining room. Arnold rubbed my shins with his furry face and Ozzy made tiny barks at me. I took a deep breath while absently petting my fur babies.

I sat there for a while, trying to process everything. Dan cared about me and yet he was forbidding me to do something that gave me a sense of fulfillment. That made me feel whole. Why was it that everyone who cared about me felt they had to tell me what to do? Why do they think they have to save me from myself? This was crazy. How could Dan care about me? Why did he have to tell me that? My emotions were a mess. I decided to go upstairs and take a shower. And a very long nap.

I woke up hours later with Arnold curled against my head.

"Hey, buddy. How's it going?"

My day was relaxing, but I can tell that yours was not. Your heart was pounding louder than Taco's squawk.

"It's been a rough afternoon." I realized by rough I meant Dan confessing his feelings for me. Funnily enough, I hadn't thought about Brad holding a box cutter to my jugular. Which just goes to show that I find it easier to wrestle with the bad guys then to deal with warm, fuzzy feelings from the people around me.

"What am I going to do, Arnold?"

Feed me some kitty treats?

I laughed. "Let's go get you some. Thanks for being my pillow."

Does that mean I get extra treats?

"Of course."

20

___

I sat eating a bowl of cereal which I thought was hysterical since I now had a kitchen where I could actually cook for myself. A knock at the door startled me mid-sip of my coffee, which, I could at least say, I had made in my new kitchen.

Aerie stood outside with her hands on her hips. "Are you going to let me in?"

"Yeah, yeah. I'm still groggy. I have a bit of a headache."

I sat at the dining room table waiting for Aerie to join me. She continued to stand over me with her hands on her hips. "Jay told me what Dan told you. And he said that you yelled at him. Are you crazy?"

I stopped mid-chew. "What?" I tried to keep the milk from dribbling out of my mouth.

Aerie sat at the table. "What is going on between you and Dan?"

"Nothing. It's the same as it is every day. He irritates the crap out of me. Only more so, now."

Aerie eyed me closely. "He told you he loves you, didn't he?"

"Don't go overboard. He said he cares about me. And then..." My voice rose on its own. "And then he *told* me I needed to stop investigating. Like he can tell me what to do."

"He told Jay that you had a box cutter to your throat. Is that true?"

"Yeah." I stared down at the bowl of cereal.

"You could've gotten killed." She reached across the table to grab my free hand.

"But I didn't. Dan showed up. And I had a tape gun that I used to its full capacity."

"A tape gun?"

"If you swing it hard enough..."

Aerie giggled. "Really?"

"A girl's gotta do what a girl's gotta do. I got away from the guy. I'm fine."

Aerie looked at me closely. "Are you sure?"

"No. I'm not fine. Dan told me he likes me. What am I supposed to do about that, huh?"

A slow grin crossed Aerie's face. "I'm sure we can figure it out."

"He still makes me so angry. How can he tell me to stop doing what I enjoy doing?"

"He doesn't want to see you dead, and neither do I."

I stuffed a big spoonful of cereal in my mouth and chewed slowly as I stared at Aerie.

"You don't want me to investigate anything either?" I said through a mouthful of Cap'n Crunch.

"No, but I can completely understand why Dan was upset seeing you threatened like that."

I stood up from the table. "Look at me. No cuts just a couple bruises. I'm fine."

"It's just that...Mira, Dan and I have both lost people we

care about." Aerie stumbled through her words. "And we don't want it to be you."

How could I respond to that? Dan had lost a surrogate family when Jay and Aerie's parents were killed.

"Okay." I took a deep breath. "I promise I won't do anything dangerous...for a while."

"Well, I guess that's as good as I'm going to get." She leaned closer. "Now let's talk about you and Dan."

The fan fell on the floor with a bang, and the kitchen window slammed shut.

We fell into giggles. Clara didn't seem to care about my love life. I wondered how we could help her.

PREVIEW OF GABLES AND GRIEVANCES

A sneak peek at the next mystery, Book #7: Gables and Grievances

The attic of my Victorian house was exactly what you would expect from a very old and haunted house. The fall day was exceptionally warm, the floorboards felt heated and the dust drifted in swirls.

Arnold had followed me. Any moment now I knew he would complain about the cobwebs.

Why is it so dusty up here? Don't you use that evil machine to vacuum?

"I'm not carrying that heavy vacuum cleaner up thirteen steps. Attics are supposed to be dusty."

Arnold harrumphed. He liked his world like he liked his fur. Impeccably clean.

This attic was far from it. It held over one hundred and fifty years of memories. And surprisingly that meant objects as well. Besides the huge wooden chest that took up the back wall, other boxes were heaped in corners. Many of them slowly sinking into decomposition. I had to clean this place out anyway, even if I wasn't here to look for clues.

"Are you up there already?" Aerie shouted from the hallway downstairs.

"Yes."

"I've brought a couple produce boxes from the diner." Aerie's footsteps caused the stairs to creak, just like a nicely haunted house should.

"Great." I pointed to the stack of ancient boxes in the corner. "Because I don't think those would make it without falling apart."

"Do you think we'll find something here?"

Arnold cleared his throat with a long meow.

"Arnold seems to think so." I laughed. But I also knew he could hear Clara, the ghost whose house I had moved into six months ago. I just wasn't ready to tell Aerie that I could actually hear Arnold in my mind. As quickly as we had become friends, I still didn't think confessing that was a good idea.

"Of all the things we've done together, helping a ghost is the craziest," she said.

"I don't know, I think jumping out of a restaurant window was pretty insane."

Aerie nodded. "Let's not do that again. Watching you twist an ankle was not a highlight." She set down the boxes. "Where do you want to start?"

I glanced at Arnold. I actually thought I caught him rolling his eyes.

She wants me to climb into that dark and dusty corner and point out which box, but I refuse to ruin the fur I took all morning to clean.

"Really? "I stared at him.

"Am I missing something?" Aerie asked.

"I guess we'll start in this corner over here."

I walked into the dark corner full of cobwebs, mouse poop, and bat droppings. Yes, bats. Although I hadn't seen any since I moved in.

"Do you have bats in your attic?" I glanced at the mess in the eaves.

"Yes, it's not uncommon in the area. Why, have you heard them up here?"

I shivered. "No. Just wondering," I mumbled. "It would be fitting seeing as Halloween is in a few days, that I should have ghosts and bats hanging out in my house."

Aerie helped me shift the pile of boxes away from the wall. "Oh, do you want to come over to make jack-o-lanterns?"

"Resounding yes, I would love to bake up the pumpkin seeds for the diner."

"Great. I'll have Jay pick up some pumpkins on his way home."

"He's living with you again?"

"Yep, he's still working on the house. He and Chelsea had another fight."

I shook my head at Jay's relationship status.

"I wish he'd officially be single and get on with it."

"Oh, I don't think Chelsea is that bad. At least not anymore. I think your brother is good for her."

"I don't know about that." She opened the top box while I took the one underneath.

She pulled out a paper-filled folder and opened it in her lap. "Electric bills from 1976."

"Yeah?"

"All I can say is wow, inflation." She put the papers back into the folder and placed it in one of the reinforced produce boxes.

We continued to look through the boxes. Most were full of folders. I pulled out the bottom box. It was severely crushed and had a dark stain of water damage, although the box was dry as a bone at this point.

I opened the box slowly, letting the dust and grime fall away from the sides as I lifted the flaps.

"Oh, what's this?" I picked up a newspaper, yellow with age and crumbling desiccated edges. *LOCAL DOCTOR ACCUSED OF PRACTICES IN THE OCCULT, sister missing.*

MORE MIRA MICHAELS MYSTERIES

If you enjoyed this story and would like to read more about Mira and her lovable cat Arnold, check out more of the Mira Michaels Mysteries.

CATS AND CATNAPPING

KEYS AND CATASTROPHES

PRANKS AND POISON

CONSTRUCTION AND CALAMITY

CARNIVALS AND CORPSES

POTTERY AND PERPS

GABLES AND GRIEVANCES

DARLA DAMIAN PARANORMAL COZIES:

MYSTICS AND MURDER

Please consider writing a review on Amazon to let others know more about Mira's adventures, please don't share spoilers! Reviews help readers find these stories which helps writers like me. That way I can continue to write what I love and create more stories for you.

Thanks bunches,
Julia

SUBSCRIBE AND SAVE!

Simply go to Julia's website at www.juliakoty.com/subscribe and add your email to our mailing list. You'll be included in our exclusive club and be the first to learn about new releases and special deals on the stories you love.

Including photos of the REAL Arnold!!

9 781939 309150